Seeds of Chaos
Book Two
-Hell's Gate-

Herbert Grosshans

Published by
Melange Books, LLC
White Bear Lake, MN 55110
www.melange-books.com

Seeds of Chaos, Book Two, Hell's Gate,
Copyright © 2007-2009,2011 Herbert Grosshans
ISBN 978-1-61235-017-2

Credits

Editor: Taylor Evans
Copy Editor: Mae Powers
Cover Artist: Mae Powers

Seeds of Chaos
Book Two -Hell's Gate-
By Herbert Grosshans

Barely escaping with his life from Eden's Gate, Thomas Stone and his two alien companions seek aid from the reptilian Srax. Unfortunately, things do not turn out as expected. When they finally end up on Ramarra, Thomas faces his greatest challenge yet. Will he find the answer to his past?

Hell's Gate is the second book in the 'Seeds of Chaos' series. The first book was published in January 2007 under the title 'Eden's Gate'. Showcase.

Herbert Grosshans also wrote the Xandra series, Daughter of the Dark, Mother of Light, and Goddess of Life. He is the author of 'Dual Visions', which contains two stories, 'Cliffs of Time' and 'Orion -- the Hunt'.

Visit him on his blog http://hegro.blogspot.com

Seeds of Chaos
Book Two -Hell's Gate-
By Herbert Grosshans

Prologue

"Commodore Stone, why did you destroy that ship full of colonists?" The deep, resonant voice of Admiral Sasmussen asked me again. I've never liked that man. There was something about him that I couldn't put my finger on. He was tall and skinny, with a haggard and gaunt looking face. His dark eyes seemed to burrow right into my skull, and his voice was the voice of doom.

And in my case, it certainly was. This man wanted to bury me.

I wasn't intimidated by his constant badgering, and I was getting angry. "Sir, as the record shows, it was not my ship that fired, even though we had sealed orders to destroy that ship. If I am guilty of anything, it would be: disobeying orders."

Admiral Sasmussen shook his head. "Commodore Stone, when are you going to stop this charade? I have a record of your orders right in front of me. You were supposed to carry out a routine inspection of the starship 'Hope' and to make sure that the ship would leave in the designated time-span. No mention of destroying it." He smiled. An executioner looked friendlier. "I signed those orders myself."

I shrugged. "Then those records are false." I said and knew how he would answer. We had been through this before.

The admiral stood up and pounded both fists on the desk. "Are you accusing me of lying, Commodore?"

"No, sir, I would never do that." I stayed cool even though I wanted to wring his scrawny neck. "I am only stating the facts as they happened and as I know them. My crew is witness."

"Your crew?" he barked. "How convenient! There is no one left."

"That's right!" It was my turn to bark. "How convenient. I demand an investigation why every member of my crew happened to be on the same cruise ship at the same time. And why that same cruiser collided with a rogue asteroid."

"Do not raise your voice in my courtroom again!" Admiral Sasmussen's voice was dangerously low. "I have a good mind to have you executed immediately. But you have friends." He gave Admiral Curtis a sour look.

Admiral Curtis, who sat beside him, said nothing. He kept looking at me, his face unreadable. He was my superior, but he was more than that, much more.

His wife, Elesia Stone-Curtis, was my adopted mother. That made him my stepfather.

"Let me give you the real facts, Commodore Thomas Reginald Stone." The voice of Admiral Sasmussen dripped with sarcasm. "Even though you had no orders to do so, you took it upon yourself to destroy the starship 'Hope', which carried 10,000 colonists in deep stasis. Ten thousand people who dreamed of a better life on a frontier planet, where they could live in peace, raise their children, and grow their own food. Ten thousand lives that you destroyed with your unspeakable act of playing god. This act brought us to the brink of war with the colonies. You claim that you had orders to destroy the ship, but you disobeyed those orders. Then an unknown ship came out of nowhere and fired the lethal shots. A ship which you had seen before on another mission ten months ago, when, after pursuing a pirate ship, you dropped into an unknown system." He looked up and stared at me. "You insist on keeping this story alive and yet--there is no record of that mission, and there is no record of any mystery ship. There are no records, Commodore Stone, not in the Fleet's computers, nor in your own ship's computer! And computers don't lie."

"The computers don't lie, but the people who program and maintain them do." I kept my voice low and calm, even though I was boiling. "I don't know what is going on, but somebody is trying to sweep something under the rug and me with it, and I will lead my own investigation to find out why."

"There will be no investigation, at least none you will head, Commodore. I recommend your dishonorable discharge from the Service. You will be stripped of your rank and privileges!" Admiral Sasmussen spoke coldly. His eyes could have frozen Hell itself. "And if you insist on pursuing your conspiracy theories I will personally see to it that you end up on some hell-hole of prison planet for the rest of your life..."

* * * *

I am a foundling. A team of researchers found me living among a tribe of aborigines on one of the planets in the *Altair System,* naked and filthy. I had no memory of my natural parents. There were no other humans living on that planet. I was either the lone survivor of a crashed space ship or the abandoned reject of a slave trader. The only language I spoke was the language of the aborigines, which consisted mainly of grunts and gestures.

The head of the team, Prof. Elisia Stone, took a liking to me and began to educate me. With the help of computers, I learned the Terran language very quickly and everything else that was crammed into my head.

A year later Elisia Stone adopted me as her son and a year after that she married Admiral Curtis.

The Admiral and I became good friends. He was like a father to me. He recommended I join the Space-force, because he saw potential in me. I rose very quickly in the ranks; I became Commodore Thomas Reginald Stone, until two months ago.

Now I was just plain Thomas Reginald Stone, private citizen.

* * * *

"Why would anyone want to discredit or even kill me?"

Admiral Curtis stared at me. "You carry dangerous knowledge inside your head."

"Like what?"

"The co-ordinates to an unknown planetary system." He leaned forward. "We want you to go to that system and find out who these people are." He smiled. "You will become a pirate."

"A pirate?"

"That's right, a pirate." He grinned. "After you got kicked off the force you were so angry that you wanted nothing but revenge. What better is there but turning to piracy." He indicated the man beside him. "Colonel Voltaire will make all the arrangements."

* * * *

So I became a pirate-merchant. After purchasing a ship, I took off on my mission to find that mysterious planetary system, accompanied by my two alien companions, twin sisters Sharina and Kabrina.

But first, we had to make a stop at Eden's Gate, to buy merchandise we could use for trading.

After making a deal with the Intergalactic Spice Company and having sex with the lovely Senjarina Dorles Rodrigo, she betrayed me and had me taken to a garbage dump.

I survived an attack by the Ghouls and was rescued by Renha, one of the Katre-people, who introduced me to her cousin, Rinca. Both of them claimed that my coming to Eden's Gate was prophesied and my union with them would produce two sons, who would lead the Katre-people into victory against the humans, who kept them as slaves.

Captured by the local Enforcers, I was charged with the murder of Dorles Rodrigo, but managed to escape my prison. With the help of Liom Valdigo, a Katre-female who had undergone surgery to make her human in appearance, I was able to board my ship and join up with my two companions.

We blasted off Eden's Gate without permission and our ship was damaged when one of the planet's defense ships fired upon us. Our life-support system was damaged in the attack. We needed to take the ship in for repairs.

The closest system was four jumps away. The inhabitants of the system were oxygen-breathers, humanoid looking, but not human. Their ancestors had been reptiles.

Apparently, they didn't like humans overly much, but we had no choice but to pay them a visit.

Chapter One

Caution is always a good policy when approaching an alien system. Kabrina took her seat at the comm-center on the bridge and waited for the moment when we would be challenged.

I sat in my chair, watching the screen, and I saw the small craft appear from behind the closest moon. When I say small, I don't really mean *tiny*. It was ten times larger than our ship, and bristling with turrets. If they weren't in a good mood our ship would make a nice new temporary star in the planet's sky, and we wouldn't have to worry about our oxygen supply.

The computer replaced the screen's view of space with the larger-than-life image of a Srax-male. He was in uniform, obviously an official.

"Approaching vessel! State your origin and your business." The voice was deep, grating.

"This is Starsurfer," Kabrina kept her voice neutral, cool. She didn't speak Srax, because there was no need. Our computer would send the transmission in the Srax-language.

"We are a human-based merchant ship. Our life-support system sustained damage in an encounter with pirates. We need assistance with the repairs."

"Am I speaking with a female?" the Srax asked. Both of his protruding eyes focused on me. "Why is the male not talking?"

I gave him a friendly smile. "I am Thomas Stone, the captain of this ship. As my comn-officer said, we need your assistance. Our life-support system could fail at any time. We have no other business with you, but if necessary we could do some trading; after all, we are merchants."

"What do you carry?"

"You are welcome to inspect our cargo," I said. "Maybe there is something that might interest you."

"I will accept your invitation, Captain Stone, but let me warn you, I will be accompanied by two armed guards." He showed large black teeth. "I've dealt with humans before, and I don't trust you."

The screen blackened for a split-second, and then we looked again into space, or at least a small portion of it. The image of the alien patrol vessel filled most of the screen. The ship rotated until we faced a huge hatch. It slid open, like the jaws of a huge shark, displaying a dark, gaping hole that swallowed us up as if we were nothing but a tasty morsel. I could almost hear the satisfied burping as the giant maw closed again.

As soon as we were inside, lights lit up to show black metal walls all around us. We were inside the belly of the alien ship.

"The air is breathable on the other side," Sharina said. "Atmospheric pressure is very close to ours."

"Well then, let's put out the welcome mat," I said, getting out of my chair. I climbed the stairs down to the lower deck, walked down a short corridor and threw open the airlock. I never trust this job to a computer.

The air entering our ship had a different smell to it. It was breathable, a little warmer, and more humid than ours was, but alien. According to our analysis, it didn't contain any toxic particles, but it had traces of unknown elements. Even though they were supposed to be harmless to humans, I felt nauseous for a moment. I took a few deep breaths to get my body acclimatized. When an oval porthole dilated in the back wall of the hangar I was almost used to the air.

The uniformed Srax we had spoken to stepped through the opening, followed by two of his guards. In their hands they carried mean looking weapons. Their leader seemed unarmed, until I saw the huge rifle slung across his back.

One thing was certain; these people were big on intimidation.

I had stepped out of our ship and stood beside the airlock to greet them. People like these craved respect and recognition. I needed their help and therefore had no problem groveling a little.

"Welcome to my humble ship," I said, standing at attention.

The Srax stopped, looked at me with his protruding eyes. His mouth opened to show his teeth. They really were quite black, but they looked strong and healthy. He gave a loud hiss; a forked tongue appeared briefly between his lips.

"I am *Flightleader Horax of the Fifth Family*, and these are my personal guards, *Hedge-Warriors of the Third Degree*. Are you a warrior, Captain Thomas Stone?"

"Not really," I smiled. "I am just a merchant. Violence is something I do not approve of."

"And yet you carry a weapon in your boot!"

"Oh, that. I keep it for my protection. I may not approve of violence, but I am quite capable of defending myself, if the need arises." No need to appear too meek.

Horax smiled again. "You don't strike me as a timid man, Captain. As I have mentioned, I am familiar with your species, and I have actually made it a point to study humans. My *Second Protector* was a merchant, like you, and he used to deal with humans. I was in his employ before I was chosen to serve our space fleet."

"Then you have the advantage, Flightleader, I know very little about your kind. You must forgive me if I don't always follow protocol."

"We are not as rigid as you may believe. You'll find that you and I are much alike." His tongue flickered across hip lips again. "Are you going to invite me into your ship or are we going to waste time out here hissing like two female egg-layers?"

"Of course not. Forgive my rudeness." I smiled. "Please, enter my ship."

He waited for me to go, and then he followed me down the corridor.

"Do you want to inspect the cargo first?" I asked as I walked ahead of him.

"Yes, I do."

He took his time with the inspection, checked everything very carefully. He also looked at our damaged oxygen-extractor. "You were lucky," he commented. "I am surprised it lasted as long as it did, but it can be repaired. I will direct you to a repair facility that is competent and reliable."

"I appreciate that. We will, of course, compensate you for your trouble."

"Good. Now, introduce me to your female officers."

The girls were waiting for us in the lounge. Both had tied back their hair into a ponytail, their emerald eyes sparkled brightly in their beautiful faces.

"You are not human," Horax said when I introduced them. His eyes swiveled in my direction. "They appear to be female. Am I correct?"

"We can speak for ourselves," Sharina said.

One of his eyes fixed its gaze on her, the other one still looked at me. A loud hiss escaped his lips. "They remind me of our own females. They also speak without waiting for permission."

I grinned. "They may not be human or Srax," I said, "but they are no different from most females. I suspect all females have the same trait."

He let out a series of gurgling sounds, and then he slapped me on the shoulder. "I think I like you, Captain Thomas Stone. Now--how about opening a bottle of that wine I saw in your storage room? It's been some time since I had human-made wine."

"Your species is familiar with the concept of alcoholic beverages?" I asked.

"Of course. Every living creature needs liquids. Discovering and liking fermented fruit juices is not unusual among life-forms."

"Among other things," I said.

He laughed again. It was quite a scary sound. If I didn't know any better I would have thought he was choking. "You and I are much alike," he rumbled. "I will introduce you to my mates. You might find them interesting."

Kabrina went to get a couple of bottles of wine and some glasses.

While the two guards didn't touch a drop, the illustrious Flightleader managed to guzzle down two bottles of our finest wine. His speech became a little slurred, but otherwise he seemed to be unaffected.

Damn it all! A good wine should be enjoyed slowly, not gulped down like so much water. He also showed way too much interest in the girls, and they didn't seem to mind at all. In fact, they drank more wine than was good for them. At this rate, our supply wouldn't go far.

"You know, my human friend," Horax said jovially, "when you take your ship down for repairs there is really no need for your officers to accompany you, is there?"

"I guess not," I admitted reluctantly, "but it is up to them."

"Oh, don't worry about us, Thomas," Sharina said, smiling at the Srax. "I'm sure Flightleader Horax of the Fifth Family will take good care of us."

Horax laughed. I winced, expecting him to choke for sure this time. Putting a scaly hand on Sharina's thigh, he let his tongue flicker across his black teeth. "I will protect you with my life," he slurred.

"I think I should get my ship down to the surface of your planet, before our life-support decides to quit," I said.

Horax rose. "You are right, of course. I will go and make arrangements for you. Without my recommendation you would have a difficult time finding a reliable repair-facility."

"I am grateful. There is one more matter: what about payment? Our money is no good here."

"What other valuables do you have, besides those spices,

11

medicines, and your wine?"

"We have rare diamonds. You may be interested in those." Sharina said.

His protruding eyes swiveled in her direction. "I might be. Show them to me."

Kabrina got up. She returned with a large cassette. It was decorated with sparkling jewels. When she opened it, I felt dazzled by the bright, purple fire glowing inside.

"Purple diamonds!" Horax said. His face was expressionless. "I have heard of them."

"We know their value," Kabrina said. "Please, don't pretend you are ignorant."

His forked tongue appeared briefly. "I admit I am not ignorant. I believe we can begin to negotiate."

His speech was still a little slurred, but the cassette filled with diamonds seemed to have had a sobering effect.

"You work out the details with my two officers," I interrupted, "just get me down to your planet."

He showed his black teeth. "I'll have the co-ordinates to the facility transmitted to your computer. I will also arrange for someone to pick you up and take you to my estate. You may as well be comfortable while your ship is being repaired."

A couple of hours later I was on my way.

Alone.

Nobody challenged my entry into the planet's atmosphere. The co-ordinates to my destination had been fed into my navigation-system, and there was nothing for me to do but sit back and relax. My new friend's family lived on the other side of the planet, and it would take at least three hours for me to reach the repair shop. I used the time to familiarize myself with the customs of these people. Unfortunately, there was not much information available, so I used most of the time to polish my language skills.

I watched the large screen that displayed the planet below. The scenery was not much different from most inhabited planets: forests, agricultural areas, mountains, deserts, and large cities. There were many lakes and rivers on the three main continents. Countless large and small islands dotted the oceans, which separated the continents.

I was surprised to find my ship heading for one of the large island.

It was in the early morning hours when I approached a landing strip. A harsh male voice asked for my identification, but I believe it was only a formality. Obviously, Horax had informed them already of my arrival, and I was expected.

The landing went quite smoothly, but I cannot take credit for that. These navigational computers are very sophisticated and do not make any mistakes. Once activated they will take a ship safely to whatever destination they are programmed to go to.

When I saw a huge service vehicle approaching, I shut the ship down and headed for the airlock.

Chapter Two

Horax had directed me to a private docking port. There was no military welcome-committee, only the service vehicle with a couple of mechanics. Minutes after I made my exit from the ship I saw a smaller air-sled approach and land.

My first few breaths of air left me gasping for a moment, until I got used to the heat and humidity, but the air was better than the stale, metallic air I had breathed inside the patrol-cruiser.

I watched the figure of a Srax in flowing robes walk toward me. A slight breeze made the thin material cling to the slim body and there was no mistaking the gender. I got a quick glimpse of a bare breast as the robe parted momentarily. A large hood that kept her face in the shadows covered her head.

She stopped in front of me, pushed her hood back a little with a slim hand and looked at me out of large, protruding eyes. "I am *Sweet Nectar*, the third mate of Flightleader Horax of the Fifth Family. You will address me as *Three*."

I bowed my head. "May your juices flow forever, Three," I said, hoping it was the appropriate response. "I am Thomas Reginald Stone. I would be honored if you call me *Thomas.*"

She opened her mouth and hissed. A long and thin split tongue played across her full lips. The morning sun reflected off her shiny black pearls of teeth. She was much prettier than Horax. "You have studied our customs," she said and looked me over appreciatively. "And you speak our language well."

Bowing again, I said, "You are most gracious, Three. But there is much I am anxious to learn."

She grabbed my hand. "Come. Enough of formalities. I will introduce you to the rest of our family. Horax told us to take good care of you." She pulled me toward the air-sled. Its top was open and I swung myself over the low partition into the passenger's seat. Sweet Nectar slid into the driver's seat, closed the transparent canopy.

Then we shot into the air.

The speed and force of the take-off pushed me temporarily pushed into my seat, before the stabilizers cut in. Sweet Nectar laughed with a high-pitched, warbling sound when my hands shot out to balance myself. "I like to fly fast," she said. "Did I startle you?"

"I have to admit, I am much more comfortable in a spaceship," I said.

"You may not believe this, but I have never been inside a spaceship." She leveled out the air-sled and leaned back in her seat.

"Do we have far to travel?" I asked.

"No, but we have enough time to get better acquainted," she said and put her hand on my crotch. Then she began taking off her robe. Her breasts tumbled out and I was surprised to see their perfect shape. Soon she was completely naked, and I stared at her most exquisite body. Fine, greenish shimmering scales covered her from head to toe; they were of a darker shade around her breasts and her pubic area. A thin, red crest rose from her round head and ran down her spine, like a hard, knobby rope.

Our seats began to decline and changed into a soft flat surface. She began to undo my clothing. I noticed that she had thin membranes between her fingers. Her mouth opened to display her black pearly teeth. "You are not familiar with our sexual customs?" she asked, straddling my exposed bottom.

"Not really," I said and moaned when her warm hand took hold of my penis. My reaction was immediate. Her warbling laughter filled the small cabin as she hovered above me, playing with my rigid member. "You human males are different," she observed. "Your organ is shorter, but thicker."

"Is that a problem?"

"Oh, no, we can adjust."

I studied her pubis. She was completely hairless. Her vulva was thick, puffed up, shaped like a heart, split in the center. She put my penis into the dark-green slit and lowered herself. The thick lips of her vagina molded themselves around my shaft as the hot, slippery walls yielded to take me deep into her belly.

She was quite tight. It was a snug fit.

She began to rotate her hips, and I watched her slim body swaying above me. Her breasts were soft in my hands, but they were firm, with thick long nipples. I had expected her scaly skin to be rough, but found it to be smooth and pliable, like soft satin.

To my surprise, I noticed that she had a navel on her flat smooth belly. She hissed softly, and then opened her mouth to emit a thin, high cry. The white collar that circled her slender neck had grown stiff; the long tendrils looked like knobby needles. I felt warm liquid running down my shaft, then down the insides of my buttocks. Her tight inner muscles milked me frantically. When she was finished, she lifted off and slid over to her seat, where she lay down on her back, her slim legs wide open, her knees pulled up until they touched her armpits. Her neck-collar had smoothed out again, but I noticed that it was still pulsing gently, its white tendrils moving like tiny snakes against her skin.

She looked at me expectantly. I rolled on top of her, my rigid penis rested on her smooth belly. Her pelvis pushed up, and I felt the strong muscles of her vulva grab my mast and hold it while she rubbed her slit back and forth. Letting out a high-pitched whistle, she pulled back a little, pushed up again. Feeling suddenly no resistance, I slid into her hot, wet sheath. Her full breasts flattened against my chest, her soft hips slammed up against mine as I slowly fucked her. She felt good in my arms, her passion matched any woman's I had ever coupled with, and her vagina, though alien, was no different from that of a human woman.

How long we were locked together, I do not know. She had climaxed several times, when a soft chiming sound emitted from the vehicle's console.

"You better finish," she whispered, "we will begin descending shortly."

The fire had been smoldering inside me and I let it flare up. With a suppressed roar, I exploded, jetting inside her with great force. She let out a trill when my hot discharge flooded her insides. Her long, supple legs wrapped themselves around my back, held me in a tight embrace until she had drained me. The tight walls of her sheath were still sucking even after I was done.

Finally, she relaxed and let her legs drop. With a hissing sigh, she pushed me off.

"I'm surprised," she said as she put on her robe.

"Why?" I asked.

"I did not expect such a virile male. Are all humans like you?"

I chuckled. "Not many are. I am somewhat unique."

"I cannot wait to tell my sisters," she said, slipping the thin hood over her head. "You will be in great demand."

The air-sled began to descend. I barely finished putting on my clothes. This was going to be an interesting visit.

Before we landed I studied the land below us, and I realized that this was one huge estate. The roofs of the dozen or so brick buildings seemed to be made from the same kind of baked clay. All were a uniform yellowish color. Tall trees and shrubs grew around every building; several small ponds reflected the bright sunlight.

We set down on a paved open space. There were a couple of air-sleds and a number of all-terrain vehicles already parked there.

"Your family must be quite rich," I remarked.

Three smiled, and then laughed with that warbling, high sound. "You are quite correct. The Fifth Family is one of the richest and influential Families on the planet. As long as we speak for you nobody will question your presence here."

She opened the canopy of the air-sled. I climbed out of my seat, stepped onto the gray pavement. The trees that ringed the landing site were much taller when you looked up.

"Welcome to our home," Three said and hooked her arm into mine. "Come, I will introduce you to my family."

We walked across the pavement toward a vine-covered archway. After passing through it, we stepped into a dark corridor. The green canopy above us did not let much light through to illuminate this natural tunnel.

The air smelled damp and musky. I saw large gnarled roots on either side of the walkway. These trees were old and huge, and judging by the sound of muted buzzing and chirping home to a variety of small life forms. We came out in a courtyard at the end of the corridor, facing a tall, sprawling building. A set of stairs made from flat stones led us to the entrance. I admired the exquisite carvings in the two wooden doors and in the thick, weathered timbers of the frame. The doors swung open as we approached, and then we entered a well-lit entrance hall.

I'm always amazed at the similarity of different species. The Srax are of reptilian ancestry, but that's the only difference. They are human-like in much of their behavior. Even many of their customs have similar ones to Earth and other planets. I was not surprised when I saw a huge chandelier hanging from the high ceiling, and pictures covering the walls. A wide staircase led to a second floor. Through an archway I saw a large high-ceilinged room. On leather-covered couches and on deep cushions on the stone-floor sat a group of women who looked in our direction when we entered the room.

"This is our guest, the human Thomas Stone," Three said loudly. "The home of the Fifth Family will be his home."

One of the women rose and approached us. She wore a long, flowing robe that covered her whole body; unlike some of the other women, who sat with their breasts exposed. They were also much younger than this one. She was quite old looking. Deep wrinkles made her face look like a chunk of material cut from the surface of an airless asteroid. She had a thin, long face, and her protruding eyes, which were surprisingly clear, peered into mine.

She lifted her arm; long, bony fingers pointed at me. "You bring the *Seeds of Chaos* with you," she said with a hoarse whisper. You will cause unrest and conflict in our family and among our people. I see death and destruction; it follows you like a plague." She turned and looked at the others, raised her voice. "Beware of this stranger from the stars. He is the harbinger of great evil." Then she stalked away, disappeared through a door.

There was a moment a silence, then Three laughed. "Don't mind her," she told me. "Old Cloudseeker has been predicting gloom and disaster ever since anyone can remember. We don't take her seriously."

The other women joined in her laughter. "Come, sit with us," one of them said, padding the empty cushion beside her.

Three waved her off. "Later, Four. Our guest has had a long journey. Let him freshen up and rest for a while. You can see him at dinner."

She was right. I felt grimy and sweaty, and my body had not quite adapted yet to the humid, hot air. Three took me down a long corridor, stopped in front of a door. "You should be comfortable in this room," she said. "It belonged to Brax, the younger brother of Horax."

"I gather he doesn't live here anymore," I said.

"Not for a long time. He was killed in a skirmish with the Sea-people."

"Sorry to hear that."

She didn't answer, opened the door. The room we entered was not very large, but roomier than any spaceship had to offer.

"There is a private cleansing room through that door," Three said. "I will send someone to scrub your body. You may want fresh, clean clothes. Brax was about your size, his clothes should fit you." She pointed at another door. "You'll find everything in there." She smiled, and then walked out of the door.

Chapter Three

The cleansing room was as expected. A water-filled bowl with a drain served as the toilet. I had to squat above it, finding it a little uncomfortable; when I looked for a lever to flush I could not find one. I need not have worried; it flushed automatically, leaving the bowl white and clean. A warm spray washed across my buttocks, dispensing all my fears. A huge tub looked inviting, but I didn't know how to fill it with water.

I had left the door to the cleansing room ajar, so I heard the gentle creaking of the hinges when the heavy wooden door to my room opened. Expecting Three to walk in, I didn't bother to cover myself; but instead of Three a young female walked into the room.

"I am Morningdancer, I am here to help you with your cleansing," she said, somewhat shyly. "Would you like me to run the water for you?"

"Please, do," I said. "I couldn't figure out how it works."

She let out a high-pitched little warble and ran her hand across one of the walls, just above the rim of the tub. Suddenly it began to rain from the ceiling. I stepped into the tub and into the rain. The water was warm and gentle. The young woman stripped off her garment and joined me in the tub. I looked at her nakedness, admiring   her nubile breasts and narrow hips.

"Kneel," she said.

I did as she told me to. The bottom of the tub was not hard, as I had expected, but soft and resilient. Morningdancer knelt beside me, ran her hands over my back. It felt good and relaxing. Closing my eyes, I concentrated on the gentle splashing of the water and soft hands of the female Srax.

Her hands moved across my buttocks, my hips. When she began stroking my belly she seemed to hesitate, then with a quick movement she cupped my testicles, squeezed them gently.

My penis stiffened, and when her fingers curled around its length, it didn't take long for me to become rock-hard. She slid underneath me, her tongue flicked across the tip of my penis, and then I felt my hard organ slide into her hot mouth. She sucked gently for a while, released me and slithered forward until her face was under mine.

"I've never been with a male," she whispered, "but I know what to do, and I am ready." Her legs wrapped themselves around my buttocks,

19

her hips lifted up, and then her wonderfully tight vagina swallowed me up. She writhed below me, slammed her hips up against mine, her lithe slim body supported only by her legs, which she had locked behind my back.

When her movements slowed, I straightened out my legs, her knees parted, and I pressed her buttocks into the soft floor. As the water pelted my back with warm, scented large drops, I fucked her with steady, gentle strokes. Her vagina had adjusted to the thickness of my penis, and I slid easily in and out of her. At regular intervals she let out a little high-pitched warbling scream, at the same time her frilly neck-collar stiffened and her vagina walls contracted tightly around my penis. When I finally felt my own orgasm approaching I put my hands around her buttocks and pushed deep into her.

Letting go, I filled her womb with my spermatic fluid. Her arms were around my neck; her slim, hot body molded itself against mine and her heels dug into my buttocks. She hissed and spit, tightening her vagina around my spurting member. Only when I was finished did she relax, her legs dropped away and opened wide. I was still hard and could have gone on, but I knew that she was exhausted. Reluctantly, I pulled out of her, willed my penis to soften.

I rolled onto my back and lay beside her, with my eyes closed. The water fell onto my face, my chest and belly, washed away the evidence of our encounter. Her hand touched my chest. I turned my head, looked at her.

She was smiling. "I overheard Three and the others talking about you. I was curious, wanted to find out for myself. Three was right, you are different."

"I thought this was your first time? How can you compare?"

"It was my first time, but I watched others. Did I do everything right?"

I chuckled. "For a novice, you did a terrific job."

"Good. Please, don't tell anyone about this. I was supposed to help you only with your washing." She sat up, straddled me. "Now, let me finish what I was told to do."

She began rubbing my chest with the palms of her hands. It didn't really help me to relax, now that I had a taste of her. Behind her back, my penis rose between my legs. When she slid back and felt the obstacle digging into her buttocks she lifted up. Hovering above me her hand reached between her parted legs and took hold of my mast. With a loud hiss, she impaled herself.

I guess I had been wrong about her being tired. Her pelvis began to rotate in my lap, at the same time she let her hips snap back and forth. If this was really her first time, she must have done a lot of watching. Her supple body writhed above me. She hissed and spit when she reached an orgasm, her split tongue shot out, impossibly long and thin, and her protruding eyes seemed to pop out even farther.

When I cupped her breasts she pressed her upper body against my hands, ground her breasts into my palms. I lifted her off me and put her onto her knees. I knelt behind her; she arched her body, pushing up tiny spines that ran down the center of her back. Parting her round buttocks, I slid my mast between them until I felt the puffed entrance to her sex-organ.

Pushing forward, I slipped into her with ease. Her hips in my hands I began to pound into her soft buttocks.

"You better finish," she called over her shoulder, "they will come looking for me."

I held her tight when I climaxed inside her. She struggled in my grasp, hissed loudly. I felt her vagina-muscles milk my spurting member until I was spent.

Collapsing on top of her, I lay on her small body. The spines on her back were soft and pliable, not hard and sharp, as I had feared. When our breathing became normal, I pulled out of her. She twisted around, turned onto her back and smiled. "You have spoiled me for life. No other male will ever measure up to you."

"You'll forget me soon enough."

"Never. I promise you." She rose, rubbed her hands over her body, and stretched her arms toward the ceiling. She had a nicely formed figure, with small breasts and slim hips. She looked fragile, but I knew better. Strong muscles rippled under scaly skin as she twisted gracefully in the spray of the water.

With a hand movement, she turned off the water. Warm air washed over our bodies, stopped blowing when our skin was dry.

Morningdancer put on her garment, smoothed it out with a few strokes of her palms. "I will find you some clothing," she said and disappeared into the other room.

Naked, I followed her. Hearing her rummage around in the closet, I flopped down on the wide bed. The mattress was flush with the floor and it was soft and comfortable. Closing my eyes, I relaxed and let my thoughts drift off.

* * * *

He was there again--the golden winged man. "The Seeds of Chaos," he said accusingly, a golden finger pointed at me. "When will you stop?"

"Not chaos," I said. "The Seeds of Life. I celebrate life and the pleasures it offers."

"Lust," he said and waved his hands in a wavy motion. "Watch."

I saw a young man, a Srax male. He was well built, muscular, with wide shoulders. His skin was scaly, the crest on his bald head high, but his eyes were wrong. They did not protrude; instead, they were almost flush, with thick lids. Human eyes.

"Your son," whispered the voice of the golden man. "This is your son."

"Impossible," I said.

"He will bring turmoil and the terror of war to three planets and beyond," he continued. "This is the gift you leave behind."

"You are lying!" I cried out. "I would never do that."

"Not you, but your seed will."

He rose on strong, golden wings. I tried to follow, but fell into darkness.

* * * *

I woke when someone shook my shoulder.

"Time to get ready," Morningdancer's soft voice said. She was bending over me, her face close to mine.

"Can your species and mine produce offspring?" I asked.

She smiled, shrugged her slim shoulders. "I don't know. There are no records, but it may be possible. We are not so much different."

"Do you bear live young or do you lay eggs?"

"We are not egg-layers. Why--are humans?"

"No," I said, sitting up. I'm just curious, that's all."

When I tried to put on my boots, she shook her head. "No boots. No footwear. We go barefoot."

She had laid out a pair of wide-legged pants and a vest that left my arms bare. After getting dressed, I admired myself in a full-length mirror and I had to admit, I struck an imposing figure.

However, I felt naked without my boots, or more precisely, the lack of my combat knife. My face was still smooth, clean-shaven. It would stay like that until I applied growth-stimulant, but the hair on my head was longer than I would have preferred. When I got back to the ship one of the girls would have to give me a haircut.

The Srax had no hair, so they obviously had no use for a comb, and

I had not brought one, either. I used my fingers to put some order into my hair and since it had some natural wave to it, I managed to make myself presentable.

Morningdancer looked me over with a critical eye and seemed to be satisfied.

"You're a fine-looking specimen," she said. "I believe you will be able to handle all the attention you will get." She smiled enigmatically and held out a slim four-fingered hand.

"Come, and remember--don't tell anyone what we did, not even Three."

Chapter Four

I expected her to lead me into some kind of dining room, with tables and chairs, but Morningdancer took me to a place outside. A number of Srax females sat cross-legged on flat cushions that were arranged in a semi-circle beside a large pool. Each held a bowl in her hands from which she took morsels of some dry food. It looked almost like puffed rice.

There was an empty cushion, and Morningdancer indicated for me to sit there. The two females on either side smiled up at me; both were young, a little older than Morningdancer; and both were practically naked. Their only garment was a little piece of colored cloth covering their genitalia.

When I looked around, I noticed that most of the others were dressed similarly. Some only bared their breasts. The only ones who where completely covered where older, one of them was the old crone who had greeted me with her accusations. She just looked at me, but kept silent, for which I was grateful. The last thing I needed was a confrontation with some crazy old woman, a confrontation I could not win.

"Ah, there you are," said a familiar voice. It was Three. She came walking around a clump of bushes, in her hands she carried a small tray, which she set down in front of me. "I had some special food prepared for you," she said. "You humans have finicky stomachs."

The other females laughed, it sounded like a flock of songbirds. I had to admit, it was not unpleasant to my ears.

Three had changed her outfit; now she was dressed in a loose, flowing robe that left her breasts exposed. She looked delicious and inviting. "I see that Morningdancer found you some suitable clothes. They fit you well." She looked at the girl who stood waiting at the entrance to the semi-circle. "I hope her services were adequate. Her behavior can be a little rebellious sometimes."

"She behaved exemplary." I smiled and looked around the circle of females. "I see no males here."

"They are only allowed at certain times. This is the *Garden of Fertility*," Three said.

"Why am I allowed?"

"You are a special guest. We do make exceptions." Three smiled, and then walked away. She stopped to speak to Morningdancer, who nodded and followed her; both disappeared through a vine-covered gate.

I looked down at the bowl on the tray. It contained some kind of black meat or fish and a vegetable stew. My cutlery consisted of a flat piece of plastic and a long needle, also made from plastic. No knife or spoon.

I speared one of the black cubes with the needle, smelled it and put it into my mouth. It was meat, and it tasted quite good; so did the vegetables. I was hungry and began to eat.

"Is it alright?"

I looked at the girl to my right, who had spoken.

I nodded. "Very good. How is yours?"

She laughed, dipped into her bowl and took some of the white kernels between her fingers, offered them to me. Opening my mouth, I let her deposit the small morsels onto my tongue. They didn't have much taste, but were not offensive to my palate, either. Swallowing, I said, "Not bad. Do you eat this all the time?"

She laughed, again. "Not all the time. Only when we get ready for the harvest celebration."

"Which is when?"

"Tonight." Her protruding eyes swiveled into my direction. "I hope you'll join us."

I shrugged. "If I'm invited. We'll see."

After finishing my food, I was longing for something to drink. As if reading my mind someone bent over me. It was Morningdancer. "You must be thirsty," she said and offered me a small tube filled with a dark liquid.

I accepted the tube, sniffed it. "What is it?"

"Juice from the fruit of the *Mist-Tree*. It has special qualities. An offering from the Lady Brightcloud. Drink it and then come with me." She watched me empty the tube. The juice had a pungent taste; it left a bitter aftertaste in my throat, but quenched my thirst. When I was finished, Morningdancer held out a hand. "Come. I will take you to Lady Brightcloud. She wants to speak with you."

We walked through the vine-covered gate, through another dark tunnel of tall shrubs and trees. When we emerged on the other side, I found myself in a small glade. Beside a pond on a flat rock sat a Srax female. She rose with fluid movements when we approached.

"I am Brightcloud," she said with a soft voice. "Horax is my younger brother."

25

She was tall and slim, dressed in a white formfitting robe. Her thrown-back hood exposed a high, purple crest. Even though the skin of her face and neck was smooth, I could tell she was not young. Around her neck, just below the frilly collar, she wore a piece of intricately carved jewelry.

"Walk with me," she said and began walking toward the tall trees. When I caught up with her, she hooked her arm into mine, as if we were old friends. Strolling down a smooth, dirt-packed path under tall, leafy trees, with an alien, but beautiful woman by my side, I felt a moment of peace. The air was warm and humid, but smelled fresh.

"Tell me, Thomas Stone, are you a violent man?"

I laughed softly, puzzled by the unexpected question. "When I am provoked I can be violent, but I prefer peace."

"You find it peaceful here?"

"Right now I am at peace," I said, "but I am a stranger here. I know nothing about your world."

"We are not a peaceful race, Thomas Stone. In a way you were lucky my brother intercepted you. Had you tried to enter our planet's atmosphere without permission our defense system would have destroyed your ship."

"Nobody challenged me."

"Because my brother had a device attached to your ship that broadcast a signal to our defense grid. You didn't know that?"

"I had no idea."

She smiled. "Others might have taken your cargo and sent you down to the surface without the protective device. But Horax is an honorable man; he is also weak, prefers pleasures to duty."

"He didn't strike me so."

"You don't know him. Unfortunately, our enemies do. He should be here, protecting the Family, not the entire planet."

"I gather you have enemies?"

"Many. The Fifth Family is one of the oldest. Our roots go back to the dawn of our recorded history. Too much inbreeding has weakened our gene pool. Horax has no sons to succeed him. My brother Brax is dead. I had two more brothers. One died as a child, the other one, Raxar, lives on *Sisson*, the fifths planet. From what I hear, he is doing quite well."

"No cousins?" I asked.

She laughed. "Plenty of them. All eager to absorb this branch of the Fifth Family. We are not ready to merge."

We had stopped under an enormous tree; four men, locking hands, could not have reached around the thick trunk. A bench of woven branches was waiting underneath the tree. Brightcloud unlinked her arm from mine, sat down, and padded the seat beside her.

There was a small pond. On its surface swam a flock of birdlike creatures.

Brightcloud let out a hissing sigh. "This is a holy place. I'd hate to see it overrun by a horde of common *Gikkas*."

"Who heads this estate while Horax is gone?" I asked.

"Our father, but he is getting old and tired. Most of the females are useless, or just not interested in the affairs of the Family. Three is the only one who keeps things organized and under control."

"How about you?"

She rose, walked to a small bush and picked some purple berries, which she put into her mouth. Her movements were fluid, graceful. One of her eyes rotated until it focused on me. "Since I do have no attachment to any male I am powerless. Some day you must study the structure of our society to understand."

"All those females I met, what role do they play?"

"Horax has seven mates, wives. The others are cousins and sisters of those mates."

"So many women and no children?"

She laughed. "Oh, there are plenty of children, all daughters, no sons." She threw a handful of berries into the flock of birds. With an explosion of noisy hooting, the birds gobbled up the tiny purple pellets.

"Would you like to go for a swim?" she asked suddenly. Without waiting for an answer she walked toward the water, dropped her robe. Naked, she stood at the edge of the pond. I caught a glimpse of fleshy, sparkling buttocks, firm, round breasts, and smooth, curvy hips, and then she dove into the water. "Come in, it is cool and refreshing," she called.

The flock of birds took flight as she intruded into their territory, circled once, then settled into the safety of the trees.

I removed my pants and my vest, folded them and put them on the bench. The water was surprisingly cool. It felt good on my skin.

Brightloud was a strong swimmer. She cut the water with great speed, aided by her webbed hands and feet. Laughing, she rose up in front of me, her breasts visible for a short moment, before she sank under the surface. Playfully she circled me, swam underneath me. I felt her hand on my belly, then on my penis. Strong fingers curled around it, released it again. Her breasts grazed my chest as she pressed her body against mine.

She shot away, leaving me panting for more. I swam after her, but she evaded me easily. Suddenly, she was in my arms, wrapped her long legs around me and began rubbing her belly against mine. My stiff member found her slit. Grabbing her buttocks, I forced myself into her. She kept us afloat by moving her arms while her pelvis snapped back and forth.

Her mouth searched mine, hot lips opened, pressed against my lips; a split tongue entered the cavity of my mouth. She tasted different, but sweet. Copulating in this position was difficult, so when I felt my orgasm approaching I didn't suppress it. With a mighty thrust I exploded inside her. She hissed into my mouth, milked me violently.

Then we broke apart. With swift strokes, she swam toward shore.

I watched her standing in the sunlight, her naked skin shimmering with iridescent colors. She was a magnificent looking woman, by any standards.

Chapter Five

I slept well that night. Early in the morning, Three came to wake me. "I have arranged a little sightseeing tour for you. I thought you might enjoy it."

Rubbing the sleep from my eyes, I stared up at her, standing there beside my bed. Dressed in a dark blue loose robe, she looked all business. "Are you my guide?" I asked.

She shook her head. "I have business to attend to, but Brak is quite capable. See you tonight."

Before I could ask who Brak was, she was gone. A few moments later Morningdancer rushed into my room. She gave me a bright smile. "I am here to help you get ready again."

Naked, I padded into the cleansing room. Morningdancer was right behind me.

"Give me a moment of privacy," I told her.

"You want to be alone?"

"There are certain bodily functions I prefer to do by myself."

"Oh, you humans are so strange. We have no such secrets."

I shrugged when she didn't move and began urinating into the bowl. She watched with interest, but did not comment. When I was done, she undressed and stepped into the shower, turned on the flow of water. I had barely joined her when she dropped to her knees, knelt on all fours, her round buttocks up. Between her slightly spread thighs I could see the strong hairless muscles of her vagina, like two pieces of soft rope.

I pointed at my limp penis. She smiled, turned and took it into her mouth. Her long soft tongue teased until I was rock-hard. Easing out of her mouth, I pulled her up, put my hands under her buttocks and lifted her on top of my swollen member. With her legs draped around my thighs she pushed back her pelvis and then forward. Even though she was extremely tight, I slid into her already creamed sex-canal with little difficulty.

Then I pressed her against the wall and began to move in and out of her with steady strokes. I didn't want to drag it out for too long, because I knew I had a long day ahead of me. When I came, I spurted with great force into her. She reached her orgasm at the same time, squirmed and hissed loudly into my ear.

When we were both finished, she rubbed my body with scented

oils. I returned the favor and massaged her little body. She moaned under my touch, wiggled her hips with sensuous movements, obviously willing to play some more. Even though I was still horny, I resisted. I knew she was disappointed, but she stood silent beside me as the warm water washed our skins clean.

She put out a pair of tight pants for me, and a short cape. When I asked if it was all right to wear my boots, she nodded. Before she left she whispered into my ear, "Remember, it is our secret."

I slapped her playfully on the rump; she smiled and walked out of the room.

Moments later a young male walked in. "I am Brak," he said. "I am your guide."

He wore a cape, similar to mine; his bare chest displayed well-developed muscles. I sensed hostility, but he suppressed it well, even managed to give me a friendly smile.

The sun was still low on the horizon and the air quite crisp when we walked across the pavement toward one of the ground cars. The dashboard sprang to life when he pressed his hand against it. The motor hummed softly as we pulled away from the parking lot. The road we took was paved with a glass-like substance that seemed to absorb the sound of the wheels.

On either side of the road grew tall trees, straight and thin. They were different from the ones I had seen in the park, but they formed a solid wall, hiding whatever was on the other side. We stopped in front of a gate. It was flanked by two towers. Two armed uniformed guards stepped into our path, another one came out of one of the towers, approached our vehicle.

When he saw Brak he waved, spoke something into a microphone somewhere on his body. The gate swung open.

"Why the guards?" I asked when we had passed through.

"To keep out intruders," Brak answered. "What other reason is there?"

"Many. To keep someone from leaving, for instance."

One of his eyes swiveled and stared at me. "Are you suggesting that the females are prisoners?"

"Not at all. Even if it were so, it would not be my place to criticize the ways of your people. By the way, how do you fit into the Family?"

"Three is my cousin." He shrugged. "She trusts me. Don't worry, you are safe with me."

The road we were traveling merged with a wide four-lane

highway. There were many vehicles on the road, traveling at high speeds.

"Where are we going?" I asked.

"So far you've only seen our females. Three wants you to experience the way *we* live, the males," Brak said with a grin. "She doesn't want you to get the wrong impression about our society."

"You don't like me very much," I said bluntly.

He focused one of his eyes on me again. "Not particularly. It's nothing personal. Let's just say, I don't care much for the human race."

"Any reason?"

"Many, but mostly one: Humans are expanding at a rate much faster than we care. You are beginning to settle in regions of space that belong to us."

"As long as a planet is uninhabited it doesn't belong to anybody," I told him.

He shook his head. "There are unwritten laws that every species should follow. There should always be a buffer zone between inhabited systems. It keeps the peace."

"I know very little about your species. The information I have does not speak with much kindness. Maybe it is time for more contact."

"We like to keep to ourselves. There is much unrest on our planet and on the others. No need to look for more problems."

Our highway merged with a super highway that had eight lanes, one way. I was surprised at the speed everybody was driving.

"Do you have many accidents?" I asked.

"You mean vehicles colliding?"

"Yes."

No. All vehicles are equipped with repulsion-devices. "No vehicle can approach another one past a certain speed. I told you, not to worry." His chuckle sounded like the coughing of a giant frog.

When I looked out of the vehicle, I noticed buildings below us. Once in awhile we would pass an exit that led to the streets below. Brak turned into one of these exits. A wall of high buildings rose up on either side of the street as we descended.

"The city we are in is called *Crystal Ray*. If you could see it from the air you would understand. I will introduce you to some people. If anyone asks you what you are doing here, tell them Government business."

He drove our vehicle into a huge underground parking lot. Then we boarded a subway that traveled at a speed I was better off not knowing. I received curious glances from other passengers, but nobody bothered us. This place was like any other metropolis; people minded their own business.

After getting off, we took an elevator back up to street level. When we stepped into the street, it was easy to see, this was not the best part of the city. We walked a short distance, and then we entered a place that had a huge sign above the entrance: THE BITING SERPENT.

A place of entertainment. One like it could be found on any planet where people searched for pleasure. Music, alien to my ears, blared from speakers. On a stage, couples gave the kind of performance that could also be found on many planets.

Naked couples--locked together in various positions.

Brak saw me looking, grinned.

"You like that?" he asked.

I grinned back. "Doing is better than watching."

He laughed, slapped me on the shoulder. "I think I'm beginning to like you," he said.

We walked past occupied tables, through a door, down a corridor until we reached another, closed door. He knocked. The door opened, a scantily dressed female let us in. The room was not very large; it held half a dozen low couches, some of them occupied. I counted two Srax males and seven females.

A large male Srax was lounging on one of the couches. On cushions if front of him sat two bare-breasted females. Both of them were quite young.

"This is the human Thomas Stone," Brak introduced me. "He is the guest of the Fifth Family."

"Thomas Stone," the big Srax said, displaying large sharp teeth. "I am, how do you humans say, pleased to meet you."

I showed my own teeth. "I might be, too, if I knew who you were."

The Srax choked out gurgling laughter, with his tongue lolling from his mouth. My first impulse was to pat him on the back, but I remembered Horax. It was hard to get used to this.

"First let me say: I don't really care much for humans, but with you I'll make an exception. I hear you are here on government business."

"Who told you that?"

"I have my sources."

"What else have your sources told you?" I asked

He settled back into his cushions. The two females at his feet ran their hands up his wide pant legs. He padded them on the head. Both girls had nice tits, not very large, but perfectly shaped. He noticed my interest, grinned. "You want one of them? Maybe both?"

"Thanks for the offer, and no offence. Not right now."

He shrugged. "Maybe later. Tell me, Thomas Stone, have you made contacts already?"

"Contacts? I am not sure what you mean."

"I don't want to pry. Have a seat." He waved to one of the females standing by the door. I noticed that the other one had a gun strapped to her waist. "Bring my guest something to drink." His eyes swiveled. "You must try our local wine, Thomas Stone."

I sank onto one of the couches. Brak sat down beside me. "He's been negotiating with someone from the Third Family," he said. "I am telling you this in strict confidence. They will deny it, of course."

The big Srax leaned forward. "Let us not play games, Thomas Stone. I know that you are here to open up trade with the Srax. I also know that you represent a powerful union of merchants. We could be of use to each other. I have connections to influential Families."

"I thought you didn't like humans?"

His tongue darted across big teeth. "I am willing to put personal feelings aside, in the interest of friendship and business."

"I'll take your offer into consideration. I cannot ignore the other offers," I said. Someone was bending over me. It was the female who had been told to bring me something to drink. I stared at her bare breasts, large and round, in front of my eyes. She offered me a long tube; clear liquid with a purple hue sparkled inside.

"Some wine?" she asked and smiled, her red forked tongue between her teeth. "Anything else you like?"

"Plenty," I said, "but right now I must deal with a business proposal."

The Srax male hiccupped loudly. "The rituals of doing business can become complicated when it is done between different species. Have you not been briefed about the way we do ours?"

"Unfortunately, there is not much I know about your species and your business practices. Competition is fierce among the human worlds, trade secrets are jealously guarded." I looked at the big Srax. "I'll be frank with you. I was sent to gather as much information as possible and make as many contacts as I can. Anyone who aids me in this is guaranteed to profit immensely."

The Srax smiled. "To understand what you are dealing with you must first understand the structure of our government. Srax is governed by ten Families. The First Family is the largest and most powerful. Then follow the Second and Third. Less powerful, but still a force to reckon with, are the Fourth, Fifth, and Sixth Family; they are also the ones most divided. The other four are there only to balance the government. All these Families are old. Over the course of time, each has split into many different branches. Horax is one branch, Brak comes from another, but both are members of the Fifth Family."

"And you?" I asked.

He grunted a couple of times. "I was not fortunate to be born into one of the ruling Families. However, times are changing. There are no ruling Families on Sron and Sisson, our former colonies. Here on Srax, there are other Families emerging who are eager to replace one or more of the weaker ones. Even among the ten Families we have power struggles going on, where one branch would like nothing better than rise higher in the power structure."

I finished my wine. The female who served me must have been watching, because as soon as I put the empty tube down she handed me another one. The wine had a strong aroma, left my throat dry and my head spinning. The female sat beside me, pressed her body against mine. I didn't see Brak. He seemed to have disappeared.

The Srax was still speaking.

"Horax of the Fifth Family," he said, "is in a position of great power, but he has no heirs. His father is getting old and Horax has more interest in his military career than the welfare of his branch of the Family. But there are other branches that are ready to step in, take his place."

"You mean Brak." I didn't make it a question.

"He told you." It was not a question, either.

"Not in so many words, but I guessed."

"You are very perceptive. Brak has won the trust of Three who would be all too happy to join Brak. She is getting tired of carrying all the responsibilities of running a Family. There is only one problem." Both of his eyes bored into mine.

"Let me guess…Horax."

He gurgled. "If he would somehow be disgraced; if it could be proven that he was trying to gain more influence by making deals with the humans without the approval of the other Families…" he let it trail.

"I think I understand." The wine was beginning to affect my thinking. I wondered what else the tube had contained, besides wine. A hand groped in my lap, soft fingers curled around my suddenly exposed penis. It grew to hardness in the female's hand. Then her mouth closed over it, sucked it deep inside. The head of my penis touched the back of her throat.

"You must follow the ritual," the big Srax said, smiling. One of the girls, naked now, climbed into his lap, fumbled between his legs. I saw a thin, long rope-like thing appear. The girl lifted up, fed it into herself.

The female in my lap released my penis, straddled my legs, facing me. Her hand took hold of my hard member, and then I felt myself swallowed up by a tight, hot and wet sheath.

The wine had been drugged, because I don't remember much about what happened. I have images of flashing, sparkling thighs, round buttocks, hot long tongues. I must have past out; when I came to my senses I was lying completely naked on the floor, with one of the two young girls moving lazily in my lap.

She smiled when I opened my eyes. Feeling my climax approaching, I groaned and grabbed her hips. With a suppressed cry, I shot my hot fluid into her. She sucked it up with the furious pumping of her pelvis.

"You are quite virile," she said when I was finished. "We've never encountered one like you before."

I looked around; there was no one else but the two of us. "Where is everybody?" I asked.

"Gone. They were getting tired. You would not stop. All the females had you. I am the only one who still had the strength to go on." She lifted off, stood on unsteady legs. "What are you?" she asked.

I sat up, shrugged. "A very virile man."

Her protruding eyes studied me with a calculating look. "I overheard the conversation," she said. "I am taking a risk talking to you. Be careful. The *Mitaar* are ruthless, crossing them brings usually death. And you signed a contract."

"I don't remember a thing," I said.

She nodded gravely. "You've had a taste of how the *Mitaar* work." She picked up a small bundle from a corner, shook it out. It turned out to be a satiny robe, which she put on. Reaching into a pocket, she pulled out an oval metal plate and put it into my hand. "Here," she said, "take this. You will be contacted."

"Who are these Mitaar?" I asked.

Before she could answer the door opened, Brak walked in, shaking his head. "You've made quite an impression. How did you know about our negotiating rituals?"

"I am a man of many talents," I said, grinning. "I hope I didn't sign my life away."

Chapter Six

Outside, it was mid-afternoon. Even though I didn't see any vehicles spewing pollution into the air, the sky above the city seemed hazy.

Brak and I had acquired a companion. The female with the gun. Now she seemed unarmed. She looked different from the other Srax females I had met so far. More muscular, taller. Pretty enough, but she didn't strike me as very feminine.

Didn't talk much, either.

We stepped into an elevator, got off at the twenty-first floor, walked down a carpeted wide corridor. Both walls were dotted with closed doors. We stopped in front of one.

Brak opened it without knocking. The door led into a huge lobby, filled with desks and computers. Every desk was occupied.

A guard barred our way. When he saw Brak, he nodded, stepped aside and spoke into a microphone on his wrist. There were more doors. One of them opened and a Srax male came out. He was old, wrinkled, but moved with grace and a haughtiness that is common to people who are used to being obeyed.

"Brak," he said and smiled. "What brings you here?"

Brak bent his head, covered his eyes for a moment, then he touched the tip of his crest. "Protector Ramax, this is the human Thomas Stone. He is a guest of your son Horax. I thought you might want to meet him."

The old man stared at me with his black protruding eyes. He had a strong chin, with a wide, thick-lipped mouth. "A human," he said. "We don't have much contact with your species anymore. Why are you here?"

I gave him a little bow, touched my forehead; hoping it showed enough humility. "My ship was in need of repairs. Your son Horax was kind enough to offer assistance."

"How is my oldest son?"

"Well enough, I guess," I said. "But I can't speak for him."

The Protector gurgled a booming laugh. "You must be a diplomat." He turned and began walking back into his room. "Thanks to my son I don't have much time, but I guess I can spare some to talk with you. Come into my office," he said over his shoulder.

We followed his invitation, waited by the door until he seated himself behind his huge desk.

"Sit, sit," he said, made a movement with his hand.

There were a couple of small couches and a chair. I sank into the chair, not caring where Brak and our silent companion would sit. Each chose one of the couches.

"Now, tell me the real reason you are here." Protector Ramax gave me a cold look.

"May I speak, Protector?" Brak asked.

"You may."

"Thomas Stone is here on government business."

"What kind of government business?" The Protector's eyes were still on me. "Are you a spy?"

I chuckled. "Of course not. I am just a simple merchant."

It was Brak's turn to laugh. "Not so simple, Protector. He is here to make contact with highly placed officials for future trading between humans and Srax."

"Is that true?"

Shrugging my shoulders I said, "I guess the secret is out. Brak here is a very sharp young man. He will go places."

Protector Ramax smiled. "I have great confidence in him. He has been a big help to Three, one of my son's mates and me. I wish Horax were more like him." He looked at Brak. "You have my permission to negotiate with this human. I trust that you will make certain that the Fifth Family will play a leading role in future dealings."

Brak touched his crest. "Thank you, Protector. Can you make that official?"

Ramax swiveled his chair around, pulled out a drawer from a cabinet behind him, and took out a sheet of foil. He fed it into a slot at the bottom of his computer, touched the screen. After a few moments the computer spat out the foil. Ramax handed it to Brak. "This gives you great power, Brak. Don't misuse it."

Brak bowed his head. "I will not disappoint you."

The Protector clapped his hands. "Now, if you will excuse me. I have business to attend to."

He was about to get up from his chair when the female, who had been silent, rose fluently from her seat on the couch, stepped up to the desk and pointed something at the Protector. He opened his mouth to speak, but a bright flash from the weapon in the female's hand silenced him. His head lolled forward, hit the smooth surface of his desk. The stench of burned flesh and bone assaulted my nose. I jumped up, grabbed the female's arm from behind, and twisted it behind her back.

"Let her go," Brak said with a sharp voice.

I stared at him; the female tried to break free. She was strong, but I pinned her upper body to the desk.

"Let her go, I said!" There was urgency in Brak's voice.

"She murdered Protector Ramax," I hissed. "You better tell me what's going on."

"He was in the way," Brak said. "Now, let's get out of here. I'll explain later. Besides, this is not your affair."

"Not my affair?" I had to chuckle. "I am an accessory to a murder. Do you think nobody will notice that the Protector is dead? We were the last ones to speak with him, the last ones in his office. They'll put two and two together."

There was a knock on the door. I held on to my prisoner, maybe I could explain myself out of this situation. Damn it! How the hell had I ever fallen into this?

"It is alright," Brak said, went to the door to open it. Two burly Srax males squeezed through the partially open door. They carried large suitcases.

The cleanup crew had arrived. This was not a murder; this had been a well-planned assassination.

I let go of the female. She straightened out, gave me an angry look and rubbed her arm. She didn't know how lucky she was. I could have broken it.

One of the newcomers opened his suitcase. I got a glance at the package inside; it looked like a body rolled into a tight ball.

It moved.

An arm reached up, a hand grabbed the edge of the lid, and then the rest of the body followed. It was a Srax male. He straightened and stretched his thin, naked body. The face looked familiar.

It was the face of Protector Ramax.

The second suitcase popped open. At first, I thought that it was another body, and then I realized it was a padded bodysuit.

The thin Srax slipped into it, smoothed out the wrinkles.

Meanwhile, the female had stripped the body of the Protector and handed the clothes to the thin man. He slipped into them. When he was dressed, he said in the voice of Ramax, "I am ready." He gave me a tight smile, his split tongue played across his lips. Looking at Brak, he said, "I hope you can control the human. I was not told about him."

"The less you know the better for you," Brak told him. "Your employment ends tonight. Forget you ever saw the human."

The two burly Srax were trying to stuff the dead naked body of the Protector into one of the suitcases, but Ramax was bulkier than his imposter, and his body not as flexible.

There was only one way they would be able to carry the corpse out of here. I had no desire to be around when they began slicing, and I was glad when Brak said, "Let's go."

Before we walked out of the door, the female hissed into my ear, "Don't speak or I'll make your tongue shorter than it already is." Her forked tongue flicked into my ear, almost like a lover's caress.

She opened the door, gave me a shove that nearly made me stumble. Nobody paid any attention when we walked across the lobby. The guard at the door smiled at Brak, touched his forehead. Brak smiled back and touched his own forehead.

When we stepped out of the building, our female companion went her own way. I watched her as she calmly walked across the street.

"What is she?" I asked Brak.

Brak gurgled. "Isn't it obvious? She is an assassin. She kills for pay."

"And you paid her?"

He laughed again. "She is expensive. I couldn't afford her. There are others involved in this."

"The Mitaar?" I took a guess and knew I was on the right track when Brak gave me a sharp look.

"What do you know about the Mitaar?"

"Enough," I said evasively, "enough to worry. I never wanted to get involved with them."

"You are now. Remember that!" His handsome face was suddenly ugly. I had to be an idiot not to realize this was a dangerous individual, not to be crossed. He was running with dangerous people. If I only knew what exactly these Mitaar were.

We didn't talk much on the way home. He dropped me off at the gate to the Fifth Family estate. Three was already waiting for me.

"I hope Brak was an informative guide," she said when I slid into the passenger seat of her vehicle.

I managed a grin. "He showed me more than I wanted to see."

She laughed. It sounded so much better than listening to Brak laughing, but it didn't cheer me up. I studied her for a brief moment, wondering how she fit into this picture.

She noticed my scrutiny. One of her eyes swiveled to look at me.

"Something the matter?" she asked.

"I wish I would have spent the day with you, instead with Brak," I said, giving her a bright smile.

Her chirping laughter echoed inside the vehicle. "I suppose I have something Brak doesn't have."

"Exactly." I grinned, putting my hand on her thigh. I felt her quiver under my touch, but she pushed my hand away, gently, smiled. "Remcor, our largest satellite, is full tonight. There will be a celebration. As our guest you are expected to be a part of it."

"I think I can take time out of my busy schedule." I chuckled. "So far I have made no other plans. Have you heard how the repairs to my ship are coming?"

"As a matter of fact, I was contacted today. They have run into a problem getting the right parts. There aren't any on our planet, so they will have to manufacture them. It may take some time." She looked at me with both eyes. "Why, are you in a hurry to leave?"

"Not particularly. I am having a great time, but then again, I am anxious to get back to my companions and carry on with our mission."

"Which is?"

I lifted my hands. "Nothing mysterious or exiting, I assure you. I am a merchant. I was on my way to fulfill a contract, when pirates attacked my ship. That is how I ended up in your system."

"I see. It proves again, the gods play strange games. Nobody knows what the reason for you coming to us may be. So, while you are here, enjoy our hospitality."

Chapter Seven

Their scaled naked skins sparkled in the pale light of the moon. Small glowing spheres floated above the dancers like giant fireflies, bathing the writhing bodies with iridescent colors.

There were six of them; they had their faces covered with veils, but it was obvious that all of them were young. Small breasts on beautifully formed slim bodies flashed in the dancing light. Round buttocks quivered, hips swayed, and flat bellies moved suggestively.

I had finished my third tube of wine and I was beginning to feel the effect. The wine had probably been laced with all kinds of endorphins and drugs to make a man shed his inhibitions. Between my legs, my penis was stiff, and I was as horny as hell.

A serving girl put another tube of wine into my hand, took the empty one away. She bent over me, whispered into my ear, "I wish I were one of the dancers." Looking up, I saw it was Morningdancer. "Why aren't you?" I asked.

She shrugged. "They are trained from very young. They can do things with their bodies no normal female can do. You are very lucky."

"How so?"

"You'll see." She slipped away.

There were others sitting on pillows on either side of me. Male and female Srax. Guests from other Families. They threw curious glances in my direction, but none of them had approached me, yet.

The dancers whirled and writhed, moving from the light into the shadows for a moment, and then appearing again in the light, closer to us. Music played from hidden speakers, sometimes softly and sometimes with increased volume. It seemed as if it followed the movements of the dancers.

On the other side of the terrace loomed a building, it lay in the darkness of tall trees. In front of it stood three chairs, also partially in darkness. Each chair was occupied by someone. I couldn't make out any faces.

One of the dancers was suddenly in front of me. She moved suggestively, beckoned with one hand.

As if compelled by some irresistible force I rose, followed her slowly as she danced back to the others. Gently she pushed me into the circle they were forming. There was another girl beside me; she was not one of the dancers. She began to undress me. I let her pull away my cape, open my pants. I felt my rigid member jump out, the girl touched it with her hand, stroked it for a moment.

Then she pulled away, began to sway her hips. I watched her like a rabbit watching a snake, waited for her to strike. A thin veil covered her face, only her protruding eyes were exposed. They shone brightly in the moonlight, staring at me without moving. She sank to the floor, writhing and swaying. Her legs separated, exposing her red painted genitals below her bright yellow belly. I fell to my knees, moved between her spread legs. The insides of her thighs shimmered with blue, iridescent colors.

With sinuous movements her arms reached out, warm fingers grabbed my penis and pulled my body on top of her.

My penis was aching so badly, I didn't need any more encouragement. With a suppressed groan I pushed forward, felt the puffed lips of her vagina open. Then I slid into her warm, tight sheath. She pushed up, took me deep into her. Her pelvis rotated beneath me, her inner muscles milked me with great urgency.

I came inside her with a roar, but she kept my rigid member imprisoned by locking her legs behind my buttocks. Her vagina felt like a squeezing vice.

Then she released me.

Slithering away, she left me aching and wanting more of her. One of the dancers danced up to me, pushed me onto my back. Straddling me, her body undulated above me. Slowly she descended, snapped her painted vagina back and forth, grazing the tip of my swollen organ with a feather-light touch, enough to drive me into frenzy. I lunged upwards, but she eluded me, teasing me. Then she sank down; hot, softly pulsing walls closed tightly around my hard mast.

Gyrating with ever-increasing speed, she made me release my sperm inside her quivering canal. A moment later she was gone; another of the dancers took her place, and then another. The music was loud in my ears; strange, alien music with a beat that kept rhythm to my snapping hips.

I was kneeling behind a pair of flashing buttocks, my hands clamped around gyrating hips, pushing my penis deep into a liquid vagina. The girl arched her back, twisted and suddenly a pair of strong slim thighs cradled me. Soft breasts flattened under my weight as I pressed my body against hers. She pushed at me with unexpected strength, slid away from under me.

One of them took my hand, pulled me out of the circle of dancers, toward the three watchers in the chairs. I saw a robed figure rise from the chair in the middle, a slim hand reached out to mine. We walked into the dark, up a set of stairs, through an open door into the dimly lit interior of the building I had seen from the other side of the terrace. I was led through another door, down a narrow corridor. The air smelled musky, sweet, like old timber. We entered a dark room. There were flickering candles on the walls. As my eyes adjusted to the dim light, I saw a huge bed in the center of the room, on the bed a great bulk, covered by a thin sheet.

There were others in the half-shadows, against the walls, waiting.

On a shelf, behind the bed, stood the statue of a winged golden creature. The body was Srax, but the face more human than Srax.

"I am *One,*" said a female voice from the bed. A candle flared up fueled by a sudden draft, briefly illuminating a face, just briefly, but long enough to make me shudder.

As if reading my mind she said, "No, I am not beautiful. I used to be. Sometimes this happens to chosen females—chosen by fate. We become breeders." Her laughter sounded like the gurgling of a male, not the beautiful musical chirping of the Srax females I had met so far. "A breeder! The gods must be laughing. My husband is never around to fulfill his duties. I have given him daughters, he needs a son. Only a son born to the first wife can inherit his title; are you aware of that?"

"I am afraid I don't know much about your customs," I said. I had trouble formulating the words; my brain seemed to be in a foggy, trancelike state.

"You will give me a son, Thomas Stone."

I managed a chuckle. "I am a human, a different species. I don't think it would work."

"It will. It has been foretold."

I groaned. Not again! What was it with these prophecies?

Somebody pulled away the covering, exposing a monstrous, grotesque bulk. Two meaty, lumpy thighs parted. They had painted her genitals with bright fluorescent colors, exaggerating the size of her vagina.

"Drink this," someone said beside me and put a beaker to my lips. The sweet liquid ran down my throat like hot fire, which spread through my whole body. Between my legs, my pole rose. I moved forward, fell between those giant thighs, and buried my face in the softness of a pair of huge breasts. I felt a hand close around my penis and then I entered a surprisingly tight sheath of hot flesh.

A shudder went through the bulky body and the hot flesh began to pulse around my hard shaft.

"I can still feel pleasure," One said and let out a soft moaning sound. "Don't be gentle. I am not as fragile as those dancers. And take your time."

I began to move forcefully in and out of her, pounding my hips against her soft, quivering belly. I became aware of a monotonous humming sound; it rose and fell with my movements. My first climax hit me with full force; I shouted hoarsely as I shuddered between the soft vice of the two meaty thighs. One pulled my body against her huge breasts, almost smothering me inside the cave they formed around my head.

My mind was foggy, but I was acutely aware of the pulsing soft walls that surrounded my spurting shaft, felt the warm liquid gush to mix with mine.

A loud cry escaped from One's lips, the triumphant cry of a predator after the kill. I remembered the black widow spider of Earth, were the female devours the male after the coupling is completed. I was hoping they didn't have the same customs here.

My pole was still rigid, so I kept on going. The statue on the shelf seemed to grow, changed shape, and became the image of the golden winged man. He came to life.

* * * *

I knew he was just an illusion, a figment of my imagination, and yet, he seemed real. There was a young man beside him, a Srax.

"This is your son," the golden man said.

"He doesn't look like me," I answered.

"You want to know what is in his future?"

I shrugged. "Not particularly."

"He will be denied his heritage; he will become a pariah, an outcast. Even his half-brother will not accept him, because he does not have the one thing that gives him status."

Only now, I noticed that he lacked the high fin that is characteristic to his species.

"But he is not weak. You gave him ruthlessness and strength; he will use it to get revenge. Watch this."

I saw explosions on busy streets. Many Srax died. Aircraft exploded, buildings were destroyed. There were political assassinations, murders of government officials.

The ten Families were fighting among each other, openly. Never before in the past had this happened. The social structure on the whole planet was weakening, falling apart.

"This is your legacy. You leave chaos behind."

The golden man's image dissolved in an explosion of lights and sounds.

* * * *

My body shuddered as I released my sperm and I could feel the strength draining away from me.

Breathing hard, I lay between two meaty thighs on top of a mountain of quivering flesh, sweat pouring from every pore of my body. I had barely enough strength to pull my limp penis out of its prison.

Somebody helped me up, led me out of the room. The walls of the dark, narrow corridor were closing in on me, and the dank air seemed without any life-giving oxygen. I needed fresh air.

My mind shut down. Like a zombie, I followed the girl who led my hand.

"I am taking you to your room." Morningdancer's voice sounded far away.

I nodded and stumbled beside her.

Chapter Eight

When I awoke, my head was clear, the previous night only a foggy memory. Morningdancer was there to rub down my body, smooth out sore muscles with her soft hands.

"It's my day off today," she said. "I asked Three if she would allow me to spend some time with you."

"To do what?"

She smiled. "To introduce you to my family and to show you how the poorer people live on Srax."

"Sounds interesting." I closed my eyes and relaxed, enjoying the feel of her gentle hands on my skin.

"I think that is enough for today," she said and stopped massaging my muscles.

I heard her walking away. Somewhat disappointed and at the same time relieved that she hadn't touched my genitals, I opened my eyes and watched her as she laid out my clothes. "I could wear my own," I said.

"Not your own. They betray your alien nature. It is better if you wear something that is not so obvious." She brought me a pair of baggy pants and a loose shirt, open in the front to display my chest.

After I was dressed, Morningdancer inspected me with a critical eye. "You can wear your boots today," she said.

It was good to slip into my familiar footwear. My hand casually touched the hilt of my knife and I felt so much better. "Where are we going?" I asked.

"You'll see. I think you will like my family. They are simple people, but honest and hardworking." She walked ahead of me, as we made our way down the corridor. I watched her slim body as she led me outside into the yard. She had put on a pair of tight-fitting pants and a loose short top, with a high collar and sleeves that ended at her elbows. She looked pretty and attractive.

As if reading my thoughts, she turned around and smiled. She slowed her walk and grabbed my hand. "Don't tell my family about us, please. They wouldn't understand."

We climbed down the stairs and stepped onto the gravel walkway. "Wait here," Morningdancer said and disappeared into one of the natural tunnels that let away from the main building.

I sat down on the steps and waited for her return. Looking around in the courtyard, I admired the tall old trees. It looked so peaceful here, but I knew that it was only an illusion. All hell would break loose as soon as someone found out that Ramax had been murdered. I couldn't imagine that his imposter could keep up the masquerade for long.

What had I gotten myself into, again? I felt vulnerable with no way of getting off this planet. I was at the mercy of people that I couldn't trust.

A soft humming sound broke into my thoughts, and then a small vehicle floated out of the tunnel Morningdancer had taken. It looked like a long sausage with handles in the front. Instead of wheels, it rested on a couple of narrow skis.

"Climb on," Morningdancer said and laughed when she saw my face. "Don't worry, it is quite safe. It rides on a magnetic field, close to the ground. And it is not very fast."

I joined her on the *sausage* and put my arms around her slim waist. "Are you allowed to drive this thing?" I asked, making myself as comfortable as possible.

Her warbling laughter echoed in the yard. "I'm not a child," she said and squeezed my arm. "I may look young, but I am a fully grown woman; you should know that, after all, you've tasted my passion. Now hang on."

We shot into the dark tunnel, much too fast for my taste. Coming out on the other side, we headed for the same road Brak and I had taken. The guards at the gate didn't give us any trouble. Maybe I was just paranoid, but somehow I had expected some. Once we were outside, Morningdancer followed the main road for a while, then she turned into a narrow, unpaved side-road. I was surprised to find that our ride was still smooth.

We floated about twenty centimeters above the ground and the small rocks and pieces of dirt that covered the road, didn't interfere with our comfort. Actually, the *sausage* was not uncomfortable at all; it was almost like riding a horse, without the gait. Morningdancer was quite apt at operating the vehicle and she was showing off her skills.

"I thought you said this thing isn't very fast?" I yelled into her ear when she took a curve with reckless speed. The road was not straight and lined with thick shrubs and tall trees, which made it impossible to see very far. Anything or anyone could be coming around the corner.

She laughed and slowed down a little. "Are you afraid, Thomas Stone?"

"I am not afraid of anything. I just don't feel like being maimed or even killed on an alien planet. What's the hurry?"

"No hurry. I just enjoy being free for a day, and I am glad you are with me." She leaned back into my arms. "I will have you all to myself. It makes me happy."

"Then let us not cut it short." I gave her a little hug and kissed her neck. "I am also happy to get out a bit, away from all the intrigue and all those women."

The thick growth and high trees gave way to shorter shrubbery and gradually stopped altogether. Then we turned into a wider, paved road, and only the odd tree grew on either side. I looked at gently rolling hills that gave the impression of a giant chessboard. Each square was covered with identical looking plants, except some squares were dark and others light. This was obviously an agricultural area.

I was correct. "We grow *Cassa-plants* here," Morningdancer called over her shoulder, but she didn't elaborate on the purpose of the plants. Once in awhile we could see buildings among the fields. Narrow roads led to them from the road on which we were traveling. We turned into one of these roads and headed for a small group of low-roofed houses.

Morningdancer stopped in front of the largest house. "This is where my family lives," she said and turned her head to look at me. "You can let go of me now, you are safe." Her warbled laughter was a delight in my ears and I could have kept her prisoner in my arms, just to listen to her happy laugh.

I smiled down at her and kissed her on the mouth. "I never felt unsafe," I said. "I had faith in your driving skills."

She laughed again, kissed me back and wiggled out of my embrace. I climbed off the *sausage* and stretched my legs. It had been just like riding a horse. Morningdancer headed for the house and I followed her slowly. She had barely reached the door, when it was flung open and a young Srax girl burst out. She jumped up into Morningdancer's reaching arm and clung to her.

"This is Morningdew, my little sister," Morndingdancer explained. "She is always happy to see me. Even though it hasn't been long since I was here."

Morningdew gave me a surprised stare. Then she whispered something into her sister's ear.

Morningdancer laughed and put her down. "Don't be scared, little sister," she said, "he won't eat you. His name is Thomas Stone and he is a human. He is a guest of the Fifth Family, and therefore to be honored. He is also my friend." She smiled at me. "A very special friend."

The little girl stared up at me with her strange, alien eyes. Then she came closer. "May I touch you, Thomas Stone?" she asked.

I gave her a reassuring smile. "Of course you may, and don't worry. As your sister said, I am not some kind of monster from outer space who eats little girls. I'm actually quite harmless and I like children. They are an important part of any family, which makes you very precious indeed."

Morningdew looked back at her sister. "He talks. Does he always talk this much?"

Morningdancer broke into a warbled laughter. "Not always. Moreover, you are not very polite, little sister. Now, let's go into the house. I want to show him off."

The little girl danced away, ahead of us. I could hear voices coming from inside the house, female and male voices, and I wondered how I would be greeted. So far, not all the males I had met had been overly friendly toward me. I didn't really expect much more.

We stepped into a large room; a group of Srax sat on cushions in the middle of the floor. They were eating. When they spotted us, they all looked up. I counted five females and three males. Two teenage females and three grownups. Of the males, one was younger; the other two appeared to be adults.

One of the older females rose to her feet. Laughing loudly, she came running toward Morningdancer and took her into her arms. "This is a surprise visit," she said, then she looked at me. One of her eyes swiveled back to Morningdancer. "Who have you brought into our house, daughter?"

"A friend, Mother. He is Thomas Stone, a guest of the Fifth Family."

"He is not Srax."

"He is a human."

By now, all of the others had risen to their feet. One of the older males came slowly walking toward us. I watched him, but there was no hostility in his face. He held out a hand.

I took it and squeezed I. "Shaking hands is not a custom of your species," I said.

He smiled. "I have studied humans when I was educated and I know much about your customs. This is one of them. I always wanted to meet a human. It is a pleasure."

I relaxed, when I looked into the faces of the others. I saw no revulsion or hostility. Only curiosity.

Morningdancer's mother came closer, then she gave me a sudden hug. "Welcome into our home, human Thomas Stone. Come, sit with us and have something to eat."

I joined them on the floor. One of the other girls brought me a cushion to sit on. I took it gratefully, and sitting cross-legged, I looked around the circle. Their acceptance of my presence puzzled me a little, but then I remembered the first time I had met the family of Horax. Except for the ranting of the old woman, none of them had given me any reason to feel unwelcome, at least not the females.

"I am Nightdancer," Morningdancer's mother said, as she handed me a bowl with some food in it. "I never asked: can your system digest our food?"

I smiled up at her. "So far I haven't had any problems. We may look different from each other, but I think inside we are much alike."

She laughed at that. Her laughter sounded as pleasant as that of Morningdancer. "Is that the philosophy of all humans?" she asked.

"I'm afraid not. Not everyone is as tolerant of others as I am. I expect it is the same here, on your planet?"

One of the males seemed to clear his throat. "You are correct, human Thomas Stone, not everyone is tolerant."

I detected a tinge of bitterness in his voice. Looking directly at the speaker, I asked, "Are you?"

His teeth shone black in his reptilian face. "Not all the time, but in your case I'll make an exception." He laughed his Srax-laugh and, even though I had heard it a lot lately, I still cringed inside, suppressing the urge to jump up and clap him on the back to keep him from choking.

The younger male beside him joined in his laughter.

I was beginning to like these people.

When they both had quieted down, the younger one said, "Maybe after we've eaten, and if my sister permits, us males can take a little walk outside and discuss some things. I am quite curious about how your species lives."

I looked at Morningdancer, who sat beside me. She reached over and squeezed my hand. "I know I wanted you all to myself today, but you go with my brothers. We'll still have the night. We don't have to get back until tomorrow." She had spoken with a low voice, but I'm sure the others had heard, because one of the younger girls let out a quiet little warble.

"I'm as curious as you. I am also interested in finding out more about your species," I said to the young male. "By the way, you never told me your names."

"Forgive us." He made a little bow. "I am called Scarl and this here is Mellas. He claims just because he is older he is also wiser than I am, but that is disputable."

Mellas laughed. "Let's not forget our youngest brother, Kayl. He may be the smartest of us all."

The young Srax gurgled and waved a hand. "He's exaggerating," he said with a quiet voice. "Mellas is the strongest and the smartest, there is no doubt. But sometimes he likes to play dumb; don't let him fool you."

"Typical male talk," one of the younger females said, "they always talk about how smart and strong they are, but what about their performance between a female's legs?"

All the females warbled, while the men only grinned.

"Hush Morningmist," Nightdancer chided, "you are much too young to talk like that. Especially in front of our guest."

The young female smiled, her black pearly teeth reflected the light coming in through one of the large   windows. "I am old enough. Only a year younger than Morningdancer." She looked at Morningdancer. "How is the human between your legs? Is he as virile as our males? How does he feel inside you?"

Morningdancer laughed. "Our mother is right; you are not old enough to speak of these things. How would you even know how a male feels inside you?"

"All this talk. Let's give our guest a chance to taste our food." Nightdancer looked at me with both eyes. "It is fruit of the *Kira-tree,* very healthy and gives a male great stamina." She put a hand to her mouth. "Oh, oh, that was the wrong thing to say."

Everybody broke into cheerful laughter. Morningdancer reached over and touched my hand again. "Welcome to my family, Thomas. They like you."

Chapter Nine

The farmstead of Morningdancer's family wasn't as fancy as the estate of the Fifth Family, but the yard was clean, the buildings well kept.

"Have you spent much time on alien planets, Thomas?" Kayl, the youngest of the three males, glanced at me with one eye, while he kept his other one on the road ahead. The vehicle we were riding on was just a platform, with four seats in the front. I sat beside Kayl. His brothers Scarl and Mellas sat in the rear seats. Behind them, the loading area was filled with sacks of plants, which I had helped to load onto the farm vehicle.

"I spend most of my time in space, inside a spaceship," I said.

"What is your profession?"

"I am a merchant. I buy and sell all kinds of products."

"Like what?"

I shrugged. "Whatever I can sell for a profit. Right now my ship is full of wines, herbs and spices."

"You are rich?"

"Some people might think so." I shrugged. "What exactly does *rich* mean? Compared to Horax and the Fifth Family I am a poor pauper."

"So are we," Scarl said behind me. "But we consider ourselves rich compared to people who live in the big cities."

"But we work much harder, too," Mellas said. He bent forward. "I've never been in space, none of us have. How does it feel to be cooped up inside a small vessel, surrounded only by an airless vacuum; knowing that at any time the protective walls of your little world might be pierced by pieces of all that debris that floats in space?"

"It is not that bad. Most of space is quite empty of anything. And we do have *repulser-fields*, which keep away the majority of the small stuff. If anything larger happens to wander into our course, our detection devices alert us and we take evasive action. Besides, much of the traveling is done in warped space anyway."

"It must be exiting to see different worlds and to meet different species," Kayl said dreamily. "Maybe some day I will be able to join our space navy and travel in space." His eye swiveled into my direction. "Maybe your and my people will start trading again and I can come and visit you on you home world."

"Forget that notion!" Scarl burst out. "That will never happen?"

"What will never happen?"

"You joining the space navy. We are much too low in the class structure."

"That may also change some day," Kayl said softly.

"I don't believe we should talk politics in front of Thomas." Mellas coughed slightly. "No offence to you, Thomas, but we don't know you, and you are a guest of the illustrious Flightleader Horax of the Fifth Family, our benefactor. Any negative talk may not be to our benefit."

I chuckled. "I may be his guest, but I have no ties to Flightleader Horax. He just happened to be the one who intercepted our course. Anything you say in front of me will stay here. I promise you that. I am quite fond of your sister Morningdancer and I would do nothing to jeopardize her or your safety." I paused. "I have already seen enough on your planet to realize that not everything here is as peaceful as it looks. Why should your planet or your species be any different from others?"

"Understand, Thomas, we are not rebels and we don't plan anything that may cause the complete destruction of our system, but there are many things which are in need of change. The rule of the ten Families needs to be restructured." Mellas spoke softly, but it was easy to detect the rebellious streak in his speech. "One of our ancestors was apparently quite high on the ladder of the Fifth Family, but intermarriage with mates of lower classes has reduced us so low, that we are almost non-existent in the family tree. Still, we are better off than most, at least we are still recognized; the majority of Srax-citizens don't belong to any of the higher Families and are therefore classless citizens, with no chances of ever being anything else."

Our vehicle had come to a halt. When I looked, I noticed that we had stopped in front of a huge storage shed. It was already partially packed with sacks filled with the same plants we were bringing.

"How about emigrating to one of the colony planets?" I asked as I jumped off the vehicle.

"We could, but this is our home." Mellas joined me. He grabbed my arm and stared at me. For the first time I noticed the scar on his left cheek. His fingers dug into my biceps. "We like it here, Thomas, and so does everyone else in our family. Horax has been a good leader, when he is around; and that is the problem. He is gone most of the time. There are others who want his position, and they will stop at nothing to achieve this. If someone else should replace him, it may not be to our advantage." He let go of my arm and turned away.

Scarl climbed off the wagon. "My brother does not always agree with our opinions. I think a change would be advantageous for us. Anything is a good beginning, it need not be violent."

"But changes usually are," I said, thinking of Protector Ramax. Changes had already begun--dreadful changes. And I was afraid that it would lead to more, none of them pleasant. "Let me ask you a question. I haven't met your father."

His eyes clouded over for an instant. "He was killed a couple of seasons ago."

"Farm accident?"

"No, bandits."

"Bandits?"

"As you already observed, not all is peaceful on our planet." Scarl followed his brother to the back of the wagon and began unloading the sacks.

Kayl, the youngest of the three brothers, gave me a pat on the back. "You would have liked our father. He was almost as big as you, and strong. Everyone respected him, and he could have made a good leader. I hope to be like him someday."

We unloaded the wagon in silence. When we were done, Mellas said, "We've taken enough of your time. You didn't come here to work. I suggest you go back into the house and entertain our females. They are anxious to talk to you." He smiled. "They may be females and soft and cuddly, but they are not stupid. Sometimes I think they are smarter than us males, but don't tell them I said that."

I grinned. "I won't. They must never learn the truth. We'd never hear the end of it."

He grinned back and broke into his gurgling laughter. I was almost sorry I had made that remark. One of these days, one of them would choke to death, after all. I wouldn't want that on my conscience. "I like you, Tomas Stone," he said and punched my upper arm. "You think like us, we are brother under the skin. Your sense of humor is no different from ours. We could get along well. I can see why my sister is taken by you."

I lifted a hand in defense. "If you're suggesting Morningdancer and I are lovers, I would like you to know, it is not so. I am fond of her, that is all."

He just smiled and walked away. I shook my head and watched him climb back onto the wagon. All three of them waved when they took off, back into the fields. I walked slowly back to the house. Looking around me at the buildings, the trees, and the farmland, it felt easy to forget I was on an alien planet populated by a non-human species. This could have been any world in the human sector of the Galaxy. Not human on the outside, but inside the Srax weren't any different from us; they were exactly like us, a fact I had to remember. The Srax lived and loved like us, thought like us, planned and schemed like us, committed murder like us. I had been witness to that.

"There you are." Morningdancer slipped into my arms when I walked into the room. She was alone, only the cushions were still lying on the floor.

"Where is everybody?" I asked.

"Doing their chores," she said and smiled at me. "Did you have a good time with my brothers?"

I nodded. "They are good men," I said.

She grabbed my hand. "Come, let us take a walk outside. The sun is shining and it is a beautiful day."

"Don't you have work to do?"

"It is my day off, remember. I am a guest here, just like you."

We walked outside. A slight breeze had come up and the sun was already beginning its downward journey, but it was warm and pleasant under the tall trees.

"What did you and my brothers talk about?"

I shrugged and chuckled. "Men-talk, you know."

"Did you talk about me?" She laughed a little and hugged my arm. She stopped and stepped in front of me. Putting her arms around me neck, she pulled my face closer and looked into my eyes. "Am I desirable, Thomas?"

"Very. Why do you ask?"

"I just want to know. You are the first male I have joined with and you may be the last."

"Why would you say that?"

"Because I am a *Protected Female*, a female without status. I can never marry a male."

"I don't understand. Your family doesn't seem to have a problem with our relationship. They seem to know that you and I have been together sexually."

"It is not my family, they don't really care, because they know that you and I will never be able to form a union. We can never be a family. The problem is our laws. Only my eldest sister, Nightmist, is allowed to start a family of her own."

"How about your brothers?"

"The same. Mellas, as the oldest male, can take a wife or two."

"What happens to your other sisters and your brothers Scarl and Kayl?"

"Morningmist and Morningdew can live either with Mellas or with Nightmist, when she gets married."

"And you?"

She sighed. "I am in the employ of the Fifth Family, and therefore considered *protected.* No male is suppose to sexually touch me." She pressed her lips against mine and molded her slim body against me. She kissed me with great passion. When we broke apart, she was breathing heavily. "I have tasted the delights and pleasure the joining of a female and male produce and I wish you would stay here forever, Thomas Stone."

"You know that would never work, Morningdancer." I stroked her cheek. "I am fond of you, but you must realize I don't love you. We don't even know each other, not to mention the fact that you and I are of two different species."

She smiled sadly. "I know. But I can dream, can't I?"

"Sure you can. What is the reason that you can't marry and have children?"

"The reason is simple. Our planet is already overpopulated. It is the only way we can keep populations down. Only the higher Families may breed freely."

"What about those dancing girls I had sex with?"

"They are sterile." She gave me a crooked smile. "Did you enjoy coupling with them more than with me? After all, they are trained for that."

"I don't remember much about last night, believe me. I was drunk and drugged. Whatever I did, it was beyond my control." I kissed her gently. "Making love with you is much more exciting and I cherish every moment we spend together."

She clung to me for a short moment, then stepped back and whispered, "Thank you, Thomas Stone from the stars, I will remember you forever."

Chapter Ten

Morningdew insisted she sit beside me at suppertime. She was the first child I had actually seen on Srax and she was a delight to listen to and to watch.

"I want to know everything you have done, human Thomas Star." She had these lovely bright blue eyes and the fact that they were protruding didn't diminish the beauty of her small face. It was exquisitely formed and covered with tiny, shimmering scales. A shame that she would never be able to break a young man's heart or taste the pleasures of love.

I laughed. "I think it would take a long time to tell you all that."

"Just a little, please?"

"Don't be a pest, Morningdew!" her mother scolded her. "Thomas didn't come to visit just with you. We are all interested in his stories, so you just have to listen."

Morningdew pouted, but was silent. She kept staring at me, though, as if to burn my image into her memory. I padded her hand and whispered, "Maybe next time you can have me all to yourself."

She gave a little warble and clapped her hands. "That would be wonderful."

"Children!" her mother said and handed me a plate with some round fruit on it. "Do you have any, Thomas?"

"Not that I'm aware of." I laughed, thinking of the visions I've had.

"Why not?"

I shrugged. "I am not married, for one thing."

"Is it against your laws?" Kayl asked. He glanced at his oldest brother. "In our family only Mellas will be allowed to ever father children and only Nightmist may give birth to any."

Nightmist let out a series of melodious sounds. "If I ever find a male who is willing to share his life with me."

I looked at her. She was quite pretty, a little taller than Morningdancer and a bit heavier. She had this habit of touching her fin when she spoke, but she was not unattractive. "With your beauty you shouldn't have any trouble finding a suitable mate," I said.

I couldn't tell if she was blushing, but I had the distinct feeling she was, because she covered her face with both of her hands and giggled.

Her sister Morningmist, who sat beside her, laughed and poked her in the ribs. "Maybe she should practice spreading her legs for a male." She gave me a bold stare. "If Morningdancer doesn't mind sharing you…" She let the sentence trail off.

"Morningmist! I've told you before, hold your tongue in front of our guest!" She looked at me with an apologetic gesture. "Forgive my daughter's bold talk. She has always been a little on the wild side."

"Only in my talking," Morningmist defended herself. "At least let me have *that*. I'll never be allowed to experience the real thing." She shrunk into herself, sulking.

The older woman beside her, who hadn't said anything until now, gave her a hug. "Don't be sad, Morningmist. There are plenty of males out there who can never marry, either, but that doesn't mean they will stay celibate. One of them will seek you out. Just be patient." She looked at Morningdew. "Go get my *tilla*; I think we need to cheer up everybody."

The little girl got up and ran into one of the rooms. When she came back, she carried an object that looked remarkably like a violin or a guitar. She handed it to the older woman, who laid it across her crossed legs.

When she began singing and strumming the strings, I was immediately enthralled by her sweet voice and her skill with the musical instrument.

Everybody just sat there and listened quietly for a while, but soon they sang along with strong and enthusiastic voices.

The music stirred something deep inside me and it actually brought a lump to my throat. In my career as a soldier, I didn't get much of a chance to listen to music and this was something I hardly experienced. Most of my life was hard and brutal, there wasn't much room for softness, and I was touched by the beauty and peace these people of another species shared with me, a stranger they didn't even know.

Morningdancer leaned against me as she sang along, her voice like the song of a nightingale in my ear. Her hand lay in mine, soft and warm. I felt like joining their celebration of life, but I didn't know the words and my voice was not used to singing. So I just sat on my cushion, closed my eyes, relaxed and listened to the sounds of peace and happiness.

* * * *

"Status report!"

"Ive spotted one of their Spy-*birds,* sir." Byrne's voice was emotionless, but I detected the wariness. Unit K had not arrived yet with enforcements. Five days of hiding inside one of the *Glass-forests* of this inhospitable planet was enough to make anyone feel depressed.

"Have we been made?" I asked.

"Negative, sir. Slovaki has done an excellent job."

Slovaki was my camouflage-man. Couldn't find a better man in any outfit.

I made myself as comfortable as was possible in the confinements of my battle-suit. The damned thing was beginning to rub my crotch sore and I was tempted to take it off, but the roots and branches of the giant *Glass-trees* would cut me to pieces in a short time. We had to get the hell out of here and find better quarters.

The air was breathable and once outside the forest conditions weren't that bad, except for the unpredictable weather. A rainstorm with the force of a hurricane could surprise us at any time. So far, we had been lucky.

After destroying one of the enemy-tanks and wiping out a troup of Vegan soldiers, we traveled on foot across the mainly hostile surface of this world, the fourth planet in the Capella System.

One of their Seekers had brought down our Jet-Lander. We were stranded here until rescue arrived.

"Captain Stone?"

I recognized Kenneth Hammer's voice in my helmet's speaker. He was our pilot, quite efficient at his job, but not much of a soldier. "Yes, Hammer?"

"Just thought you'd like to know, we are running low on rations."

"Tell me something I don't know."

"I just finished the rest of my water."

That wasn't exactly news either, but it reminded me again that we had to get out of here. There was plenty of water available in the many rivers. Processed and sterilized it was quite acceptable. That wasn't the problem; the problem was getting undetected to the river. The Vegans had set up camp only a few kilometers away from our position. They had moved in after we had taken refuge in the *Glass-forest*, otherwise they would have detected us as soon as we entered their range.

One of Byrne's tiny spy-satellites had reported the arrival of the Vegans only a day after we had made ourselves comfortable inside the forest. Three *Tanks* and a couple of small *Transporters*. The Saurians were settling in for a long stay.

"Can you take out that *eye*, without betraying our presence, Roberts?"

"Affirmative, sir. I mean, I can try."

If Roberts couldn't do it, no one could. "There is no room for mistakes, Roberts. If you fail, we're toast. They'll destroy this whole forest just to find us."

"I know, sir."

Sometimes you just have to have faith, and I had faith in my men. They were the best. I crouched down beside Byrne, who was watching his screen. He was zooming in on the *spy-eye*; it was sitting in the top branches of the giant iron-tree we had passed when we headed for the protection of this forest five days ago. We could see the tiny pencil with the *eye* on one end slowly rotating on its axis. It had a 360-degree radius and an object approaching from any direction would not escape detection, unless it moved with the speed of light. It would be easy to send out Slieman, he'd have no problem blasting it out of the tree with his Mark-Seven, but he'd also be spotted and would hand the Vegans our location on a silver platter.

"I've tracked its movement, sir," Robert's voice came calmly over the comm. "It's an easy target."

"Then go ahead and do it!"

We watched the drama unfold on Byrne's screen. It was actually quite anti-climactic, not as much fireworks as the one Slieman took out. The whole process was not really great marksmanship. Roberts sacrificed one his tiny spy-satellites by maneuvering it close to the *eye* and detonating it above it. The result was just a small explosion, but large enough to destroy the enemy spy bird.

"It's done," Roberts reported, but we had already known.

We had to get closer to the Vegan's camp before they discovered their spy-eye gone. We knew from experience that they were overconfident in their ability to keep enemies away from their camps and sloppy in setting up surveillance systems.

"We'll move out at sixteen hundred hours, that'll give us enough daylight to reach the foot of the mountain range north of the enemy camp, where we can hide inside the caves." We knew about the caves from earlier reconnaissance flights, before the Vegans decided they wanted in on the discovery of the *Mecka-crystals*.

We had thirty minutes to get ready. More than enough time. There wasn't much to pack, except for the surveillance systems and our weapons. We were traveling light. Most of our stuff had gone up with the destruction of our Jet-Lander.

The plan was to sneak up on the Vegan's camp und destroy it. It sounded like a suicide plan, with just the six of us, but it was feasible. Once inside their safety perimeter, they'd never detect us, until it was too late. Roberts and Byrne recalled their little army of spy-satellites. We broke camp and moved out of the Glass-forest.

The alien sun was already close to the horizon, bathing the barren landscape with its silvery light and throwing long shadows ahead of us. An airless moon couldn't have been more desolate.

We made good time and arrived at the foothills shortly after dark. Locating a suitable cave was easy; there were plenty of them cut into the hard yellow rock. After checking it out for animals that might be lurking inside we made ourselves comfortable. It was quite warm inside and I decided to take off my battle suit. The others followed my example, except for Slieman, who took the first watch at the entrance to the cave.

"When is Unit K supposed to be here, Captain?" Hammer sucked on his empty canteen, shrugged and threw it onto his folded suit.

"Your guess is as good as mine," I said laconically, watching Roberts, my weapon specialist.

He had emptied his huge backpack and was taking stock of his arsenal of weapons. He looked at the pilot and grinned. "Are you in a hurry to get off this lovely paradise, Hammer?"

"Aren't you?" The pilot lifted his hand. "On second thought, don't bother answering. You'd be happy in Hell. I mean, where else would you get a chance to play with your toys?"

"You're wrong, my friend. I'm as anxious as you to get away from here, but you're right, I'm looking forward to do some damage first. We can't let our scaly friends have this planet--not without a fight."

I chewed on an energy tablet. Not exactly gourmet food. "We'll look for water in the morning," I told Hammer. "We might find some in the other caves. Now, let's get some shut-eye."

* * * *

There are moments just before you wake up when your dreams become the most lucid--the ones you remember. When I opened my eyes, I expected to see the dark damp walls of a cave around me and feel hard ground underneath my back. It took me a moment to realize I was lying in a soft bed. Snuggled against me the warm and soft body of a woman. She moved in my arms when I shifted my weight. Inhaling her sweet fragrance, I closed my eyes again and drifted off into an uneasy slumber.

* * * *

It hadn't been too difficult to penetrate deep into the enemy's camp. Surveillance was non-existent and we had moved in the next night under cover of darkness. They didn't even have any sentries stationed outside of their barracks. Slieman and Roberts were setting up their toys that would entertain us with some nice fireworks. Their targets were the *Tanks* and the *Transporters*.

They detonated nicely, lighting up the night spectacularly. We didn't give the Vegans a chance to find out what had woken them from their sleep. Before they could gather their wits, we blew open the doors to their sleeping quarters and burned them as they tried to get into their battle gear. They never had a chance.

War is not pretty, people die. After a battle, remorseful feelings start accusing you of the terrible thing you've done. You see the faces of the men you've killed. The fact that they weren't human doesn't make it any easier. Not human, but intelligent beings, with families at home. Wives and children. Brothers and sisters. Parents.

"Why do you want to murder me?" Her protruding eyes pleaded with me. She carried a child in her arms. It looked at me with human eyes. The child lifted a hand, reached out toward me.

"No!" I cried out. "This is not what happened."

"Chaos!" a voice boomed from the darkening sky, "You seed chaos..."

I woke to a silent room. The place beside me was empty. As I was about to sit up, the door to the room opened and Morningdancer walked in. She was already dressed.

"You looked so peaceful in your sleep," she said, smiling, "I didn't have the heart to wake you. Did you have pleasant dreams?"

Pleasant dreams, indeed.

I sat up, wiped the sleep from my eyes. "It is too early to get up," I said, "come back to bed."

"I wish I could," she said, "but we have to go back today. I want to enjoy the rest of the day with you, but not in bed."

Chapter Eleven

After saying goodbye to Morningsdancer's family in the evening, we headed back toward the Estate of the Fifth Family. It was dark by the time we passed the gates and Morningdancer dropped me off in front of the large entrance door.

I went straight to bed, and for a change I had a quiet night, without any nightmares. In the morning, Morningdancer was there again, as usual. She seemed subdued, moody. I didn't ask why. We didn't have sex.

After breakfast, another Srax girl came and told me to follow her. We went outside, walked down a by now familiar path in the shade of tall trees and shrubs.

When I stepped into the small glade by the pond and saw the robed figure sitting on the bench under the giant tree I expected Brightcloud, but when she turned and threw back her hood I realized it was someone else.

"I am *One*," she said as I came closer. When she saw my startled look, she laughed with a soft chiming sound. *"One of the Fourth Family.* I am sister to Brightcloud and Horax."

"May your juices flow forever, One," I said, bowing my head. "I assume you know my name."

"I was intrigued when I heard that a human was a guest of my brother's family, and watching you at the Fertility Celebration really aroused my curiosity."

"You saw me with the dancers?"

She smiled. "Not just the dancers. I saw you with One, everybody did."

"How?"

"We do have the means to transmit images and sounds across great distances. Sending a hologram from inside a building to the outside is no great feat."

"I don't remember much about that night. My body and my mind were drugged. I know there were a lot of candles, a bed and a huge female. But they may have been an illusion. Drugs do that to a mind." I said.

"Your memory is not so bad." She laughed; her long tongue appeared briefly between her lips. She rose from the bench, took the cloak she had been sitting on and spread it on the ground. Then she sat on the cloak, invited me to join her.

She looked at me out of her large protruding eyes. I noticed that they were of a bright blue color.

"You are in danger," she said with a low voice.

"What do you mean?"

"You were given an object. Do you have it with you?"

I groped in my pocket, pulled out the small, oblong plate. "You mean this?"

Nodding, she held out one four-fingered hand. "It is a communication's device. I'll show you how to use it."

I handed it to her. She squeezed the sides with her thumb and forefinger. It split open, then she closed it again. "All you have to do is open it and speak. It will connect you directly with me." She pressed it against the back of my hand for a moment, gave it back to me.

"That girl, who gave it to me, she works for you?"

She nodded.

"You have nothing to do with the Mitaar?" I asked, watching her face.

"No. And neither should you."

I chuckled. "I know nothing about them."

"I know you don't. The Mitaar are a threat to our way of life. They want to overthrow the rule of the Ten Families."

"Who are they?"

"Criminals. Outcasts. Some of their leaders come from distant branches of the Ten Families. The Mitaar pray to a deity they call *The Golden Warrior*, a winged being, a god."

"I think I've seen the statute of that god in the chamber of One. Last night. Then it was not my imagination." I said.

"One is not a member of the Mitaar, as far as I know; there are others, outside that organization, who also pray to the golden god."

"Very interesting," I said. "That cult has a huge following on the human worlds." I studied her silently for a moment, wondering. "Why are you telling me all this?" I asked her. "Why would you care about my welfare?"

"We used to have more dealings with humans." She in turn studied my face. "Suddenly, here you are, at a time when there is unrest and trouble on our planet. Do you believe in omens and prophecies?"

I shrugged. "I believe in facts. I make my own destiny."

"There are things beyond the control of us mortals, they happen, if you want them or not. Why did you come here?"

"To have my ship repaired."

"No other reason?"

"No other reason, despite what you may have heard." I decided not to lie to her.

Her eyes stared into mine. "You may believe that, Thomas, but I think that you are the pawn in some scheme unknown to you. I think you will bring changes to my species. Not all good."

I laughed. "When I first came to this family, there was on old female who carried on about disaster and unrest, which would be the result of my visit here. Don't tell me you believe in that stuff."

"What I believe is not important. What others believe, is." She smiled and touched my hand. "But now, let us talk about other things-- with our bodies." With that she opened her garment, exposed her breasts. Her arms went around my neck, pulled me toward her bosom. I kissed the deep cleft between her ample breasts, moved on to take one of her nipples into my mouth.

"That's good," she murmured.

Her garment opened farther; soon she lay naked underneath me. Pushing my pants down to my knees, I lay between her soft widespread thighs. With a grunt I practically forced my stiff mast into here extremely tight vagina. I slid in with unexpected ease; her insides were already moist and slippery, and hissing softly into my ear she pushed up against me.

For a while, she went utterly wild, twisting her sinewy body beneath me, hammering her hips against mine until she experienced her first orgasm. Her long tongue entered my mouth, curled around my own tongue.

I brought her to another climax, and then I released my own built-up pressure, shot my sperm into her welcoming vessel.

We disengaged. I stripped naked, made her kneel on the cape. Then I entered her from behind. The soft spines on her back stood stiff as she arched her body, gyrated her hips. She had lovely, full buttocks; they shimmered with iridescent colors in the light of the morning sun that filtered through the branches above.

I was suddenly aware of soft hooting coming from the pond. When I looked, I saw the flock of large birds becoming agitated. Flapping their great wings, they created small waves on the quiet water of the pond.

"I think someone is coming," One said with a breathless voice. She pushed back against me, took my penis deep into her. I took my cue and with a shout, I emptied myself into her again. She bucked and hissed, and then she relaxed with a sigh.

We were still joined together, when I saw a shadow beside us. Pulling out of One, I turned to face the intruder.

It was a young female. She looked at my erection, and then she fell to her knees beside One. "The First Protector of the Fifth Family is dead," she said. "They are waiting for you."

One sat up, one of her eyes swiveled to look at me. "It is beginning," she said softly, and then she turned her attention to the girl. "Thank you. You may go."

The girl bent forward, kissed One on the forehead, rose and walked away. She looked back once, her eyes on me, and then she disappeared into the darkness of the path.

"What do you mean: It is beginning?" I asked. "You don't even know what happened."

"The First Protector, my father, was old, but healthy. Either he died of an accident or he was murdered. I will find out."

We dressed. I would have liked to take a dip in the pond to wash the sweat off my body, but it would have been inappropriate.

"This is family-matter," she said, "but as a guest of my brother, and the Fifth Family, you may accompany me."

I didn't argue. I was curious myself.

Brightcloud came to greet us when we walked into the meeting hall. She had her hood thrown back to expose her bright dorsal fin. She looked drawn and agitated.

"What happened?" One asked.

"We are not sure. They found his dismembered body floating in the Silver-River this morning. Brak is trying to find out more."

"Brak?" One said and hissed. "I don't trust him."

"He is cousin to Three, and he *is* of the Fifth Family," Brightcloud said and lowered her voice. "He has been a favorite of the First Protector, tread carefully."

"Are you forgetting? I am *One of the Fourth Family*."

"How can I? You constantly remind me of it." Brightcloud smiled to take the edge of her remark.

One put her hand on her sister's arm. "Has Horax been told?"

Brightcloud nodded. "Three has spoken to him, as is her duty. He will arrive tonight."

I wondered if he would bring Sharina and Kabrina with him. I could sure use a couple of familiar and friendly faces right now. A heavy weight was beginning to take shape inside my guts. Something nasty was about to happen, and I had the foreboding feeling I was going to be part of it.

There were seats set up in a semi-circle, facing a speaking platform; most of the seats were occupied. I saw mainly females. The few males who were present were all servants, except for Brak and a couple uniformed Srax, law-enforcement officers, I suspected.

Three was standing on the speaking platform, addressing the small crowd. "We don't have details, yet, but as soon as we know more I'll let you all know. Until then, go and carry on with your usual duties."

She looked around, spotted us by the door and hurried to greet us. She shot a quick look at me, but said nothing.

"I'm told Horax will be here tonight," One said.

Three nodded and said, "Hopefully he'll know what his priorities are, after all, he is now First Protector of Branch 27 of the Fifth Family."

"He knows where his duties lie," One said, a little too frostily, I thought.

Three looked at me, and then pulled me aside. "I'm sorry you are drawn into this, Thomas. I had hoped we could spend more time together." She spoke with a low voice.

"I had hoped the same," I answered and gave her an inquiring look. "I assume you know that Brak took me to meet with the First Protector, or didn't he tell you?"

"He did. Brak and I have no secrets."

Looking into her eyes, I realized only now that they were purple. She had no eyelashes, and her lids were almost white. She had them half-closed, and I wasn't sure if she knew the truth already. Was she involved? I wasn't going to assume that. If she was, I could be in trouble.

"I guess I won't see much of you after Horax arrives," I said.

She gave me a little smile. "Who knows. We'll see. Much can happen."

"You must be the human I was told about," said a male voice behind me.

I turned to stare into the narrow face of a Srax male. One of the uniformed law enforcers. His protruding eyes looked at me with a cold expression. I noticed the oversized laser gun he had strapped to his hip. I gave him a big smile. "I guess, I am. Unless another human has landed here in the meantime."

"I've never liked humans," he said coldly.

"Why not?"

"You are an arrogant, fast breeding race. You act as if you own the stars."

Brak appeared beside him. "Now, now, Eyemaster Rexor, don't be so hard on our guest. He has shown us no reason to hate him." Brak said jovial and slapped the enforcer on the back in a familiar gesture.

"Not yet," Eyemaster Rexor said.

Brak chuckled. "Rexor is my cousin. Don't take him too seriously."

"I may be your cousin, but I represent the law," Raxor said bristling and stared at me. "Guest or no guest, human or Srax; anyone who breaks the laws, I will go after them. Remember that."

Chapter Twelve

Flightleader Horax of the Fifth Family arrived late that evening. He brought two of his Hedge-Warriors with him, but not my two companions.

When I saw him I addressed him as *First Protector*, but he waved me off. "Officially I am still Flightleader. I won't be First Protector until after the ceremony." He lowered his voice. "I am not even sure if I want the position."

"How are my shipmates?" I asked him.

He grinned, displaying his large black teeth. "If you are asking: Did they miss you? I have no way of knowing. I took good care of them. Do not worry. How are my wives?"

I grinned. "Are you asking me if your wives missed you? They probably did."

"Have you been treated to your satisfaction?"

"I am very satisfied." I smiled. "You have beautiful and gracious wives."

Horax laughed so loud, I thought he would choke right in front of me. Even his bodyguards grinned. "You are a diplomat, Thomas Stone. You must have met my first wife, One. She used to be beautiful, tall, slim, and fragile. More beautiful than any of the others. But now she is so ugly that I don't even want to think about her."

He turned away, stared at a tall statue in the corner of the room. I recognized the image of the First Protector, his father. "She worships a winged, alien god, The Golden Warrior. She believes that he is going to appear in the flesh someday and give her a son. The son I couldn't give her. The son she couldn't give me." He chuckled. "Even a god wouldn't want to put his seed-spout into her diseased flesh." Turning, he looked at me. "Would you?"

I shrugged. "I am not a god. What do I know what a god does."

"How are the repairs going?" Horax asked, changing the subject.

"Apparently they ran into problems with parts. But they promised me it wouldn't take much longer. I am anxious to be on my way." And that was no lie.

"You are welcome here as long as you like. We will talk more tomorrow. By the way, I notice you are still carrying your weapon in your boot. Don't you feel safe here?"

"I feel quite safe, thank you. I guess it is just out of habit," I said.

* * * *

That night Three came to my bed. When she slipped under the covers in the darkness, I didn't know it was Three, but I suspected it. She pressed her nude warm body against mine and kissed me hungrily. Then she pulled me on top of her, spread her legs wide and drew up her knees. I slid into her with ease, fucked her in this position for a long time.

When she finally spoke I realized who she was, but I had already suspected it. "No male of my species can last as long as you. I will miss you."

I had been on the verge of coming. Grabbing her by her shoulders, I entered her as deep as I could and with a hoarse shout, I exploded inside her. She wrapped her long legs around my quivering buttocks, pulled me against her until I was dry.

"I thought you'd be with your husband tonight." I said, lying beside her, trying to catch my breath.

"We abstain from coupling when we mourn."

"Then, why did you come to me?"

She flopped onto her belly, propped herself up on her elbows. "The First Protector was not my father. I am not in mourning." Climbing on top of me, she rode me with a wildness she had not before, and then she left. I slept quite peacefully after that.

A loud banging against my door awoke me in the morning. Before I threw back the covers, the door was pushed open and a group of uniformed Srax rushed in, their weapons drawn. Among them the two Hedge-Warriors.

Their leader, Eyemaster Rexor, pushed the barrel of his weapon into my face.

"Human Thomas Stone, you are under arrest for the murder of the First Protector."

I sat up, suddenly wide-awake. "You have the wrong man. As a matter of fact, it was a woman, an assassin, who shot him."

Rexor held up a familiar object. "Is this your knife?" he asked.

"I don't know," I said. "It looks like mine. Where did you get it?"

"We found it buried in the First Protector's chest."

"Impossible. He was shot, not stabbed. Check my boot; my knife will be in its sheath."

One of the Hedge-Warriors brought my boots. The knife was gone.

"This is not a Srax weapon. It is a weapon used by humans. Since you are the only human on our planet it is clear: You are the murderer."

"I told you, I didn't do it. That murder happened three days ago. The knife was still in my possession last night. Flightleader Horax even commented on it. Ask one of his guards?"

"So you admit you had this weapon with you when you were in the office of the First Protector."

"Of course I did. But I still had it with me when I talked with Horax. Why don't you ask him?"

Eyemaster Rexor gave me a hard look. "I would, if I could. First Protector Horax is dead, murdered by your hand, with this weapon. But you know that already."

When I tried to get up, he hit me in the chest with the butt of his rifle. It knocked the breath out of me for a moment. I lay on my bed staring up at him, counted the weapons aimed at me.

Three ugly looking rifles and two pistols, just as mean looking and without question just as deadly.

Five hard alien faces, five pairs of protruding eyes focusing on me--and my only weapon was in the hands of my tormentor. He held it pressed against the barrel of his gun. The fool had no idea what that weapon really was, and I wasn't going to enlighten him.

The darkness was gathering inside me, it sent cold shivers up my spine. The coldness crept into my brain, made me see things with a clarity I only had in the face of danger.

I could have taken the knife away from him, killed him with an upwards sweep. I would be among the others before they knew what was happening. But that would have been stupid. I had no way of getting off this planet. I needed help. I needed friends. Killing these five males would get me neither.

So I smiled, suppressed the pain in my chest, moved carefully when I sat up.

"No need to become violent," I said. "I am innocent of this crime. What motive would I have to kill Flightleader Horax? I don't repay hospitality in such a way."

"We have methods to find out why you did this. For now I am satisfied to know that you are guilty." Eyemaster Rexor stepped back. "Make sure he doesn't escape," he said to his companions. "I have things to discuss with Brak."

When he turned away, I noticed something I had not seen before. Rexor had a tattoo right behind his flat ear, the tattoo of a winged creature.

Pieces of the puzzle were beginning to emerge.

One of them tied my hands while the other three covered me with their weapons. They weren't taking any chances. The darkness inside me had subsided, and with it the certainty that I could have escaped. "Let me at least put on my pants and boots," I said.

It is not easy to slip into a pair of pants with your hands tied behind your back, but I managed, with the help of one of my captors.

Before they led me away, Morningdancer came rushing in. She cried out, "He was with me last night, all night. He is innocent."

I smiled at her and said gently, "It is alright, Morningdancer, you don't have to cover for me. I didn't murder Horax, and the truth will come out."

Morningdancer clung to me. "Don't hurt him," she pleaded. "He is the father of my child."

One of the law-enforcers kicked me in the ribs. "You've coupled with one of the *Protected Ones*. You are without morals. You will be executed for this."

They pulled Morningdancer away from me, pushed me through the door. I heard her wailing in the room, someone closed the door, shut off the sound. I was hustled out of the house, into a waiting aircraft. When I looked back, I saw Three standing in the dark tunnel that led to the house. I wondered why she hadn't come to talk to me before they took me away.

The aircraft lifted, shot away toward the city. It was a beautiful day outside, hot and humid, as usual. I would have liked to go swimming in the pond, make love to Brightcloud or to her sister, One of the Fourth Family, or even Three. I remembered last night, our passionate, wild lovemaking.

She must have been the one who had taken my knife. Had she killed Horax, her own husband? If not Three, who?

Brak had been at the house. He had been present when the First Protector, Ramax, was murdered. Obviously, he was involved.

I still wasn't sure about Three.

Remembering the tattoo I had seen on Eyemaster Rexo's neck, I had the strong feeling that he was part of this. He probably had ties to the Mitaar, like his cousin Brak, who was cousin to Three.

Another thought popped into my mind. "Tell me," I addressed one of the law-enforcers, "is Eyemaster Rexor related to Three of the Fifth Family?"

"They are brother and sister," he answered, and then he glared at me. "I don't have to answer your questions. Don't talk anymore."

"I know all I need to know," I said. I felt stabs of regret, disappointment. Three had seemed so sweet. *Sweet_Nectar*--her real name. She should change it to *Poison Nectar*.

We landed on top of a tall building. An elevator took us down to the 22nd level where they threw me into a holding cell. There was a bunk and a hole in the floor. On the wall above it a waterspout. This brought back memories of another cell I had been in just a short time ago.

There was one difference: this time I didn't have my disrupter, and I was on the 22nd floor.

Sitting on the bunk, I contemplated my situation and came to the conclusion that it did not look good. An alien planet, my ship in repair, my companions in space, with no idea what was happening to me, accused of a murder I hadn't even committed--and all the evidence pointing in my direction.

It didn't take a genius to figure the odds against me.

And yet--as long my body was breathing, there was hope. I remembered something. Groping in my pockets, I found the little device the girl had given me. I flipped it open. At first, nothing happened, then the little screen lit up, began to expand. A shadow appeared, took shape. I looked at the three-dimensional image of One of the Fourth Family.

She wore a loose fitting robe that hid the lovely shape of her body. Her face was unreadable when she stared at me out of her bright blue eyes.

"You must have had a reason to give this device to me," I said.

She nodded. "I did."

"Whatever it was, I'm grateful I have this communicator. You may be my only hope. There is no one else I can turn to, or trust."

"I'm told you murdered my brother," she said.

"Why would I do such a stupid thing? Your brother offered me his help, opened his home to me. We had a business deal. I don't murder my business partners."

"I know you didn't murder him."

"Then you believe me?" There was hope after all.

"It is not a question of belief. That little device you have in possession is more than just a communicator. It tracks the movements of the one who possesses it. You never left your bed that night, and Horax was murdered in the middle of the night, when you slept."

"What else does this device tell you?"

"That you spent most of the night with a female."

"Was she the one who stole my knife?"

"No. While you were coupling with her someone else, a male, crept into your room and removed it from your boot."

"Who?"

"I don't know." She smiled. "The device is not that sophisticated."

"At least you know now that I am innocent. There is no reason anymore for them to keep me imprisoned."

"I wish it would be that easy. There is more here at stake than just your life, Thomas Stone." She closed her eyes for a brief moment. When she spoke again, she averted her eyes. "I will try my best to keep you from being executed. They say you are a spy."

I laughed. "I am not a spy; just a man who seems to fall from one disaster into another. I am beginning to believe in these ridiculous accusations that bad luck follows me."

She gave me a little smile. "You must be a favorite with the gods."

"How so?"

"Perhaps you're being tested just to see how strong you really are." She shrugged. "How can we mortals understand the whims of the gods." She made a motion with her hand. "Be patient."

Her image collapsed, the screen went black. I closed the small device, shoved it back into my pocket.

There was nothing to do but wait.

Chapter Thirteen

A guard brought me some water and a bowl of a thick soup. No cutlery.

In the afternoon, Eyemaster Rexor came for a visit. He had two mean looking colleagues with him. Before he said a word, he hit me in the stomach with his fist. I think his fist hurt him more than my belly, but he didn't let on.

"You'll be transferred away from here," he hissed into my ear. "Let me give you a warning: keep your mouth shut. If you talk too much something bad might happen to Morningdancer and your unborn child. And if you believe that your shipmates are safe in space, you believe wrongly. They can easily be brought down."

After kicking me again, this time with his foot, all three of them left.

It was not long after that when five uniformed Srax came marching down the corridor. A guard opened my cell door, ordered me to come out. After shackling me, I was escorted back to the rooftop, where we all boarded a big, black, sleek-looking aircraft.

Moments later, we were airborne.

These guys were really paranoid. Why else would they shackle me to a bar above my seat? Unless I could grow wings, there was no place for me to go, not from a few kilometers up in the air.

Since I had nothing else to do, I made myself as comfortable as I could. I even slept a little. My cell had no windows. I realized we had landed when I didn't feel the vibration under my butt anymore.

One of my guards threw a hood over my head to cover my eyes; then they hustled me, as fast as my shackled feet would allow, into a building.

I knew we were inside a building by the echo of our footsteps. It took me by surprise when, instead of into an elevator, I was pushed into an antigravity shaft. Floating down a hole, without being able to see anything was a little disconcerting. But I landed easily on my feet; my guards were right beside me.

I was marched down another corridor. The soft *whoosh* of a door told me that we had entered a larger room, which was confirmed when the hood was pulled off my head.

Momentarily blinded by a bright light I blinked, let my eyes adjust. There were five Srax in black robes sitting at a table, with their backs toward a large window. The sun, which was low in the sky, let me see only dark silhouettes.

It was a cheep trick, designed to impress and intimidate.

I made a mocking bow and said, "If I could see your faces I could use the correct form of greeting. But I don't know if I am in the presence of men or women."

One of the two guards spoke for the first since I had been taken into custody. "Speak only when asked," he said harshly.

"It is alright," said one of the five behind the table. He spoke with a deep, resonant voice. Suddenly it was not as bright in the room; the sun was beginning to disappear behind a tall building. Overhead lights illuminated the five Srax.

They were old, their faces wrinkled, but all of them had clear, sharp eyes.

"I am Prime Protector of the Fourth Family. You are Thomas Stone of the Human Federation. You have been accused of a serious crime."

"That is correct, but I am innocent of the crime."

"So you say. All evidence seems to contradict you."

"Not all evidence. There is evidence which supports my claim." I paused. "But you probably are aware of that. Why else would I be here?"

"There are rumors that you are a spy," one of the Srax said.

"Rumors." I smiled. "Another false accusation."

"Why are you here?"

"I'm sure you have been told."

"We have, but you tell us in your own words."

I had no reason to lie. They were probably scanning me right now. Everything I said would be registered and evaluated by a computer. "My ship was damaged when we were attacked. Your system was the closest and most logical to search out for repairs. Flightleader Horax of the Fifth Family intercepted us when we approached your planet. He offered assistance in exchange for merchandise. I had nothing to gain by murdering him."

"We were told that your mission here was to gain intelligence about possible trade."

"Brak of the Fifth Family made up that story. I just went along with it."

"What is your relationship with Brak?"

I shrugged. "He showed me the city."

"Are you aware that he is claiming the position of First Protector? A position vacated with the death of Horax."

"I was not aware of that, but I am not surprised. Even though Horax had not been declared First Protector, yet."

"Only a formality. With the murder of his father he was the successor."

"Have you found the murderer of First Protector Ramax?"

"Not yet, but we will. Have you any knowledge that could aid our investigation?"

Was that a trick-question? Anything I said was under scrutiny. How to answer? "Would it matter if I had?" I said casually.

"Then you have information?"

"I didn't say that. How can I trust any of you? I don't really know who you are. For all I know you could be members of the Mitaar."

There was a moment of silence.

"We are not. I am Prime Protector Ramaar of the Fourth Family. To my right sits Prime Protector Myrax of the Fifth Family and to my left Prime Protector Mortar of the Second Family, Prime Protector Sprock of the Third Family and Prime Protector Extor of the Sixth Family. I assure you, we are not the Mitaar. We are the High Council of Srax."

"I must be of great importance to you if you take time out of your busy schedule to deal with me," I said dryly.

"Anything which concerns the security of Srax is our responsibility," said Prime Protector Mortar. "Right now we don't need any interference from the Human Empire. Our two sister planets Sron and Sisson are threatening to break free of the home planet. We cannot allow that. Any contact with humans at this time may upset the delicate balance of power. You understand?"

"I understand. I am not interested in creating conflict among the Srax. If I can just have my repaired ship, I will leave your system as soon as possible. You will never hear from me again." I meant every word I said.

"We believe you," Prime Protector Ramaar said slowly, "but we cannot take any chances. You have been in contact with the Mitaar; we do not know what you have learned. Our scans tell us that you speak the truth, but we do not know enough about humans. You may have the ability to control your thoughts and reactions. You realize we cannot allow you to leave our planet alive?"

"Are you telling me I will be executed?"

"Not executed. Erased from existence."

"Same damn thing! I am innocent of any crime. Is this how you treat all of your visitors?" I shouted.

"Not all of them, only the ones who pose a threat. And you, Thomas Stone, are a possible threat."

"Possible threat? What about my companions?"

"They'll be brought down and dealt with."

The darkness rose up inside me again, gave me clarity and a sudden insight. It gave me the ability to control my thoughts, my nervous system, and my facial expressions. "You are right," I said with a cold voice. "I am a spy. I came here to gather intelligence about your species, your defenses, your weapons, the size of your space fleet, and details about your way of life."

Stunned silence followed my *revelation*. One of the Prime Protectors, Extor of the Sixth Family, rose, pointed a finger. "Then you admit that the Human Federation is planning to invade our system?"

I shrugged. "I am just a simple spy. What do I know. I can tell you this, if you kill me you'll have an armada of warships here in a matter of days, but you won't have to worry, because you won't be around."

"What do you mean by that?"

"I have a device inside my head. It is a powerful bomb. Any attempt to remove it will detonate it. Killing me will detonate it. Unless you give me assurance that I will leave your system alive, I will detonate it myself. When it quits transmitting my superiors will know that I am dead. They will assume that I have been found out and that the Srax are hostile toward the Human Empire."

"You are lying!"

"It is true, about the transmitter," said Prime Protector Mortar. "It is transmitting on an unknown subspace frequency."

"And the rest?"

"True, also."

"We cannot risk a confrontation with the humans," Prime Protector Sprock said.

"We cannot let him leave. This is a dilemma." Prime Protector Extor looked around the table. "This is a decision for the Supreme Protector."

"There is no need to involve the Supreme Protector. We can handle this." It was Ramaax of the Fourth Family who spoke. "Apparently he has fathered a child, maybe more than one. Humans are very protective about their offspring. There will be no war with the Human Empire, he will see to it." His eyes swiveled, came to rest on me. "Am I correct, Thomas Stone?"

I smiled. "You have discovered our weakness. We humans are quite possessive when it comes to our children. We will go out of our way to protect them. If you let me go free I will convince my superiors that the Srax are a peaceful species, and hostile acts would not be in the best interest of both our races." My smile grew wider. "I would only be telling the truth. I have grown quite fond of all the members of the Horax family."

"Especially the females," Prime Protector Sprock said. I couldn't tell if he was sarcastic.

"What about the murder of Horax?" asked Myrax. "Someone needs to be punished."

"May I make a suggestion?" I said.

"Speak."

"I am not saying that Brak and his cousin Eyemaster Rexor are involved, but it may be a good idea to begin your investigations with them. Who knows what you will discover."

"We will take it into consideration."

"One more thing: can I have all my things back? Especially my knife?"

Prime Protector Ramaar looked at the guard beside me. "See to it." He waved his hand. "Now go. May the Guardians guide you."

Chapter Fourteen

A Srax male I had never seen before came to pick me up from my prison. He didn't wear a uniform, therefore he was not a law-enforcer, and neither was he a guard.

"I am Rek," he answered my unspoken question. "I am in the employ of One of the Fourth Family. She gave me instructions to take you to a safe place."

"A safe place?" I chuckled. "Is there such a place for me on this planet?"

He gave me a curt look. "You are protected by the Fourth Family. No one will dare touch you. I promise you that." He touched his side and smiled thinly. The gun on his side was huge and menacing. "No one!"

He led me to a large black aircraft. It reminded me very much of the one that had brought me here. I wasn't really overly excited when I boarded it. How did I know that I could trust this guy? However, I had really no choice. I was at the mercy of anyone who offered me help.

Before I sank into the seat beside Rek, I was surprised to find a bundle on the floor. He saw my astonished look and chuckled. "I took the liberty to recover your property. It's all there, even your weapon." One of his eyes swiveled in my direction as he strapped himself in. "Feel free to check it out."

I smiled at him. "I trust you. I hope I won't find any reason ever to use it on your planet. I am a peaceful man."

His laugh was not reassuring. I don't think I'll ever get used to it.

"I assume we are not going back to the Estate of the Fifth Family," I said.

He shook his head. "You assume correctly. Since Flightleader Horax's demise the Fifth Family is not obligated or in a position to offer you protection." He glanced at me and turned back to his controls. The soft humming inside the cabin changed its pitch as he took us into the sky. I was happy to see the building I had been held prisoner in fall away underneath us.

"You are fortunate that Lady Nightcloud has taken an interest in you," Rek said.

"Lady Nightcloud?" I asked.

"One of the Fourth Family. That is her real name. You didn't know?"

"I didn't, but the name does make sense. I know she is the sister of Brightcloud. Both are sisters of Horax. I'm slowly beginning to see some kind of pattern in the names. Are you related to anyone I know?"

"Who do you know?"

"Good question. Brak, for instance."

"Brak," he repeated slowly. "Cousin to Sweet Nectar, the third wife of Horax, and, of course, cousin to Eyemaster Rexor. Yes, I know who Brak is. Soon to be First Protector of the Fifth Family." He didn't look at me when he spoke. "Not a man to be crossed. He has powerful friends."

"He's a criminal," I said.

"As I've said: he has powerful friends. Tread carefully around him and watch what you say."

"I hope our paths never cross again." I picked up my bundle and began opening it. "Do you mind if I change into my own clothing? I'd feel much more comfortable."

"Go ahead."

I climbed into the back. There was large open space where one could walk around. I put on my shirt and hung the cape around my shoulders, then I changed into my own tight-fitting pants. Before I slipped the knife into its place in my boot, I balanced it in my hand. I felt its warmth and watched the blade come to life for a brief moment.

A man should never be separated from his weapon. Ever.

"I guess you and Brak are not related, am I correct?" I was standing close behind him. Even his big gun wouldn't protect him if I didn't like his answer.

"I am a member of the Fourth Family. Brak and I are as far apart as you and I. Our genes have nothing in common." He turned his head and looked at me with both eyes. "Put away your weapon, human Thomas Stone." His teeth shimmered like two rows of black pearls between his thick lips. "Even if you should manage to kill me, you would never survive. This vehicle responds only to me. If I should suddenly stop emitting signs of life, it would turn and take you back to the prison I just rescued you from." He indicated the seat beside him. "Join me in the front and relax until we get to our destination."

"A safe place," I said and sheathed my knife. Then I climbed back into the front.

He shook his head. "Not that I blame you, Thomas Stone, but you must learn to trust someone. Not everybody on Srax is your enemy."

I closed my eyes. Might as well take his advice and relax. Nothing else to do.

We landed inside a small glade. Beside a pond stood a cottage-like building. It looked peaceful.

No one came to greet us as we climbed out of the aircraft. He held out a hand. "This is as far as I go."

I shook his hand. He had a strong grip. Too bad I didn't get a chance to know him better. There was something about him--he radiated honesty and an inner strength, and I had a feeling there was more to him than he led on.

"The dwelling is open. There is food and drink inside, and a comfortable bed to sleep on." He smiled. "Much better than your last one. Someone will come for you in the morning. You'll be safe, only trusted people know about your presence. Stay safe and may the Guardians protect you."

He turned and boarded his vehicle. I watched him take off and disappear over the treetops. Then I slowly walked down the gravel path toward the cottage.

He was right. I found food on a table and a pitcher of wine. However, before I ate, I needed to wash up. I felt grimy and sweaty, so I stripped and, naked, I walked to the pond and jumped in. The water was cool and refreshing.

I floated lazily on my back and stared into the blue sky, wondering what Sharina and Kabrina were up to right now. They must be wondering about me, and possibly worry.

They didn't know, of course, about Horax. What if his men in the Guard-ship had been notified about his death? Would the girls be safe without their protector?

I didn't want to think about it.

Later I lay in the soft grass and let the alien sun dry my body, then I went back into the cottage and sat at the table, eating the by now familiar food and drinking green-colored wine.

When the pitcher was empty, instead of feeling good, I had fallen into a miserable mood.

Damn! I missed those girls. I had grown fond of them and if something happened to them, I would feel responsible. I should have never left them alone.

I spent the night in a comfortable bed, but suffered from loneliness and was extremely miserable.

What could be worse than being stranded on an alien planet with no friends? Especially female friends.

* * * *

The happy chirping of birds woke me up. I felt actually rested and quite content. Amazing what a good night's rest can do for you.

Before I got dressed, I took another dip in the pond. I was just climbing back on land, when I heard a soft humming. Then I saw it: a small aircraft descending from the sky.

Cursing silently, I watched it land. My clothing and my knife were in the cottage, too far for me to get in time. I breathed a sigh of relief when I saw the person disembark from the aircraft.

Smiling, she came closer. She looked as beautiful as the day by the pond, when I had seen her for the first time.

"Lady Nightcloud," I said and made a little bow.

She laughed and stepped up to me. "No need to be so formal," she said and kissed me. Then she stripped off her gown. Her body was as lovely as I remembered it. She put a foot into the water. "I haven't had my morning swim yet," she said and dove in.

I watched her as she cut the water with powerful strokes. When she turned around to float on her back, I caught a glimpse of the smooth and strong muscles of her genital area.

She came back and lithely she jumped onto shore. Dripping water, she stood in the morning sun and let the cool breeze dry her naked body. She saw me watching her and, laughing, she said, "Let's eat first. I've brought breakfast."

Chapter Fifteen

She was as passionate as the first time, when we had sex on her cape beside the pond. She had invited me to her private chambers. Her husband, First Protector of the Fourth Family, was at work in his plush office in the city.

"Come," she said, smiling, beckoning me with her finger. She lay naked on top of the wide bed, her thighs open in invitation.

"You are insatiable," I said and turned away from the large window overlooking a large pond and a beautifully landscaped garden. I moved between her spread legs, entered her without preliminaries. She was ready, hissed loudly into my ear as I began to move.

The Srax males have longer, thinner penises, and the first time I had entered her she was extremely tight, but after coupling all morning her vagina had adjusted to the size of my member.

She seemed starved for sex and couldn't get enough of me. My ability to go on for hours fascinated her, and she was determined to wear me out.

Her neck-collar flared and her breath was coming faster. I knew she was on the verge of another orgasm. Speeding up, I grabbed her buttocks. She hissed, pushed up against me. The pressure inside me had been building up, and with a shout, I vented inside her. Relaxing in my arms, she let out a series of small hisses, caressed my nose with her long tongue.

"I will miss you," she said. "No male has ever made me feel this way. It is time we have more contact with the human race."

I chuckled. "Not all human males are like me. Apparently I am an unusual specimen."

Her protruding bright blue eyes stared into my face. "You are unusual in many ways. As I told you before, your presence here will cause changes to take place." She shuddered slightly, her hand went down to her belly, stroked it gently. "Somehow I will be part of that change. I know it is not possible, but I can almost feel your seed growing inside my womb."

"Our species may not even be compatible," I said. "Not to mention, it takes some time for the fetus to become detectable."

She laughed, her fingers dug into my buttocks. My penis was still inside her, half-erect. Contracting her powerful inner muscles, she squeezed until I was rigid again.

"I want to produce offspring with you," she said, "so let us make certain."

Her lower torso moved underneath me with sinuous movements, her alien vagina milked me until my engorged penis pumped its load into her again, leaving me drained and exhausted. I lay on her bed, breathing hard while she straddled me, laughing down at me. "Don't tell me you are already giving up," she said, playing with my limp member.

"I think I need some time to recuperate," I said. "Your appetite is almost greater than mine."

"Being number one wife doesn't mean that you are also number one with your husband when it comes to copulating. Sometimes a husband prefers his younger wife." She pressed her slit onto my penis, began to rub it slowly back and forth. I stared at her strutting breasts; they sparkled with glittering colors in the rays of the sun shining through the large window. Her long tongue played across her shiny black teeth. She hissed loudly, let out a series of high-pitched shrieks and doused my thighs with her warm liquid. Around her neck, the purple collar was swollen and rigid.

Watching her in the throes of an orgasm had its effect on me. Thrusting upwards, I penetrated her easily, made her squirm above me. Her belly rippled as she rotated her hips faster and faster in my lap.

She lifted up. Bending over the bed, she presented her plump buttocks. I entered her from behind, kept thrusting until I filled her womb with my sperm one last time.

This time I was really done and collapsed on top of her. My chest heaving from exhaustion and gasping for air, I cradled her shaking body in my arms.

After awhile she stirred and wiggled out from underneath me. "Will you join me for a swim?" she asked.

"I'm too tired," I said. "I'll watch you through the window."

She didn't even bother to dress. Naked, she stepped through a door into the garden. Lying in my bed, I watched her walk toward the pond, admired her slim, lovely figure. She moved gracefully down a graveled path, stood with high-stretched arms beside the pond. The sun's rays bathed her with a golden light, highlighting her full breasts and round, plump buttocks. On top of her head, her crest stood high and proud, creating the illusion that she was taller than she actually was.

Looking back, she waved, and then she dove into the water.

I turned onto my back and closed my eyes.

* * * *

He was tall and handsome. He had inherited the beauty from his mother and the gray eyes from his father.

Half human, half Srax, he was stronger, smarter, and more ruthless than any of his peers.

The First Protector of the Family knew that he was not his son, but he was the son of his First Wife; and that gave him the right to inherit the title of First Protector.

He was not the only half-human born. There were three others, two males and one female. One was a pariah; he lacked the high fin that made him Srax. The other one had been born to a *Protected* female, who was without status.

The female was the daughter of Brightcloud. Beautiful beyond description, and just as ruthless. Her eyes betrayed her ancestry--almost Srax, but not quite.

He made her his wife, his only wife, against all traditions, even though she was his cousin and half-sister.

Their ambition caused war and turmoil between the Families, changed ancient laws and turned order into chaos.

"The Seeds of Destruction are inside you," said the voice of the Golden Winged Man, "and you keep spreading them."

"I have no control over it," I said.

"You have, it is always your choice."

"Why do you keep haunting my dreams?" I cried out. "What do you want from me?"

He smiled sadly. I saw that he was standing in some kind of force field, immobile, unable to move.

* * * *

A soft hand touched my shoulder, woke me from my dream. One smiled down at me. She was still naked; droplets of water clung to her shiny skin, like sparkling diamonds. Her split tongue darted serpent-like between her black pearls of teeth.

"Did I exhaust you this much?" she asked, laughing. "You should have come to the pond with me. It is rejuvenating. Come, I will have a feast prepared for us. You can meet some of the other wives."

"I wouldn't mind a shower first," I said.

Her cleansing room was similar to the one I had used when I was a guest at the Fifth Family Estate.

One joined me in the shower, rubbed down my body with her soft hands, while the water sprayed around our naked bodies. She laughed delightedly when she saw my erection, sank to her knees and took my penis into her mouth. After that, she bent backwards until her hands touched the floor, pushing out her hairless slit. I stepped between her spread legs, put my hands under her buttocks for support and penetrated her offered sex-canal.

Her hips and buttocks moved furiously in my grip; she was supple and had great endurance. When I came, she straightened out her upper body, put her arms around my neck and wrapped her legs around mine. Her tongue darted into my mouth, probing my palate. Hissing softly, she squirmed in my grasp, and then she untangled her limbs from mine.

"You are very strong," she said. "Most males of my species become weak in their knees when they loose their seeds."

I laughed, bent forward and took one of her nipples into my mouth. She squirmed against me and hissed into my ear.

We finished washing and dressed.

"When Brak takes over the position Horax held he will be one of the First Protector's of the Fifth Family," I said.

One nodded. "As long as it can't be proven that he was involved in the murder of my brother, yes, he will be the new First Protector of Branch 27 of the Fifth Family."

"What about Horax's wives?"

"They will become his property."

"Including One?"

She laughed. "Including One."

"And Brightcloud, your sister, what's going to become of her?"

"I have made arrangements for her to live here."

"Good. She is a good person."

"She is. But now, let us have something to eat."

We had a great dinner. I was getting used to Srax food. The other wives were charming, and they showed a lot of interest in me, but I didn't get a chance to sample them, much to my regret. There were some good-looking females among them. The First Protector of the Fourth Family had great taste.

Apparently, my ship was finally ready. The next day One took me to the repair facility; she accompanied me when I checked everything out.

The storage rooms were empty. There had been a cost overrun.

When I protested, One told me that it was out of her hands. There was nothing she could do.

"You have to make concessions, Thomas. It took all my persuasive powers to get my husband to arrange your release from prison."

There were some crates, which had not been there before, in one of the storage rooms. One smiled when I noticed them. "There are a few things I can do," she said. "I was told that your supply of food was running low. I took the liberty to have your stores replenished. I hope your companions like Srax food."

"When they get hungry enough they will." I chuckled and then cursed loudly when I realized that my precious wine was also gone. Those bastards! To take a man's wine, that is low. They hadn't left me even one bottle.

"What will I drink?" I asked.

One pointed to a crate. "Our wines may not be as pleasing to your palate as your own, but they are considered excellent on all three planets in our system." She smiled. "You seem to have enjoyed your share of Srax females, I'm sure you'll enjoy our wines."

Grinning, I bent forward and placed a kiss on her lips. "I enjoyed very much," I said.

When we came to my bedroom she asked, "Are these your sleeping quarters?"

I nodded. She removed her garments and lay naked on the bed. "This is my only chance to ever copulate inside a space-vessel. It stimulates me." She smiled, opened her arms. "Come, this will be the last time you and I can be together."

When I entered her, she hissed softly into my ear. Her strange, protruding eyes never left my face the whole time we moved against each other. Even though I was in a hurry finally to get off this planet, I took my time.

It was late in the afternoon when we were both too exhausted to carry on.

"May the Guardians guide you safely on your journey," she said formally when I kissed her goodbye, and then she climbed down the short flight of steps. Before she got into her air-sled, she turned and waved. I waved back, remembering another woman a short time ago, on another planet.

I waited until her sled was a tiny dot in the distance, then I locked the hatch, walked slowly back into my control room. The co-ordinates of the moon, where the patrol vessel was stationed, were still in my ship's computer. My only fear was that I may not be able to leave orbit unchallenged, but I need not have worried. I left the planet behind me without much fanfare, watched the huge sphere slowly recede.

Leaning back in my captain's chair, I closed my eyes and listened to the soft, familiar music coming from the speakers in the ceiling.

It was time to forget about the women I had left behind and think about Sharina and Kabrina. I felt a little guilty; they hadn't been much on my mind ever since I left them with Horax and his crew.

Two females, alone on a ship full of lonesome males. All of them probably young and horny.

Damn it, I had to get there fast. Who knows what trouble they could get into.

Chapter Sixteen

The girls never asked about what had happened down on the planet, and I didn't want to know any details about their stay on the patrol vessel. When I told them about the death of Horax both of them fell silent for a moment.

"He was a man misunderstood by his family," Kabrina said.

Sharina blinked a few times. Her strange, emerald eyes were large and shiny when she looked at me. "We are glad to have you back, Thomas. Even though Horax assured us you were in no danger, we feared for your safety. We should have been with you."

She came up to me and looked into my eyes, smiled and kissed me. Her tongue snaked into my mouth, and then she broke away. "Did you miss us?" she asked. I saw her needle-thin fangs and wondered briefly how Horax had reacted to their poison.

"As much as you missed me," I said.

Kabrina giggled and looked up from her comm-station. "That much?"

"That much. Now--what do you say we break open one of those crates and sample that wine I brought. I hope it is comparable to the stuff they stole from us. Did any of you check the food?"

"I did," Sharina said and smiled. "You must have made some friends down there. If the wine is as good as the food we have some pleasant hours ahead of us."

After we had eaten and emptied a couple of bottles of Srax wine all three of us were in a playful mood, and we played. On my wide bed. They fed me their aphrodisiac, and I didn't fight it, let it flow through my veins, enjoyed the tremendous orgasms it produced. After all the females I had coupled with on Srax, lying in Sharina's and Kabrina's arms, I realized I had actually missed them. Could it be I had fallen in love with them, or was it just the poison they injected into me?

Was I even capable of loving anyone? Then again, did it really matter? After exhausting ourselves, I slept, sandwiched between my two lovely companions; their bodies warm and soft against mine.

* * * *

Folding his black, velvety wings around his golden body, he looked at me and smiled. "They tried to stop me, you know, but they failed. My sons and daughters are everywhere, spreading their seeds. Chaos will rule."

Laughing, he spread his wings, soared into the black sky.
* * * *

The ringing of the alarm over the comm. woke me from my dream. Sharina was already up. Kabrina stirred beside me, sat up, rubbing her eyes.

"It's just the computer letting us know that the capacitors are fully charged," Sharina said.

"Who really needs to know?" Kabrina complained. "I'm still tired."

I could have done with some more sleep myself; I had not slept well. My dreams were becoming increasingly more disturbing. What did they mean? The winged golden man was not real. He was a myth, a legend, a religious figure. And the so-called Guardians? My adopted mother, Elisia Stone, was an archeologist and had studied ancient ruins on many planets. She had found no evidence that there ever existed a race of immortal super-beings who had ruled the Galaxy, or that members of them were still among us.

"Are you getting up today?" Sharina asked when she saw me lying on my back, staring at the ceiling.

I turned onto my belly, studied her lovely form. She was already dressed in her tight-fitting bodysuit. "I had forgotten how beautiful you are," I said.

She laughed. "I'm not coming back to bed."

"Your loss. How about you, Kabrina?"

Kabrina stuck her head out of the bath-cubicle. "It is tempting, but we've lost enough time already. Don't you think you should finally feed the co-ordinates to our destination into the computer, Thomas?

"In good time, but first I want to find out where exactly we are."

"Don't you trust us, Thomas?" Sharina gave me her innocent-little-girl look.

"Frankly, no," I told her bluntly. "I've been disappointed by too many people--people I trusted. I don't take any more chances." I jumped out of bed and walked up to her. "The truth is everyone who knew the co-ordinates has died, except me. I care too much for your safety."

She smiled. "Nice try, Thomas."

We had made a couple of jumps since we left the Srax system. Before we went into the next series of jumps, I wanted to make certain all our systems were functioning properly. But Kabrina was right; it was time to give the computer directions. We couldn't keep jumping haphazardly through the Galaxy. We were still in explored space, and our destination lay far beyond that. I gave the computer the co-ordinates and put the navigation system on automatic.

Then we readied ourselves for the jumps. Our ship was not designed for long jumps; it was really only built for short hops between systems. A trip like the one we planned would tax its resources to the limit--and ours. The computer told us we could reach our destination with eleven jumps. Two months real-time, one week ship-time. A patrol ship, like the one I had commanded, could make it in less than half that time; but this was only a luxury cruiser.

Jumps bring visions and nightmares. Multiple jumps would make them worse. The girls never told me what they saw, but when I suggested we use the stasis pods, they agreed. We would spend most of the time in dreamless sleep. If anything happened during the jumps, we would never know about it—or care.

Not every ship is equipped with Stasis-chambers. Whoever had been the owner of our ship had spared no expense. Actually, the chambers were only meant for emergencies. Sometimes ships get lost or brake down, leaving travelers with few options. One could commit suicide by opening all exists, that was the fast way; or one could wait for the food and water to run out, that was the slow death.

On the other hand, one could go into stasis and hope that another ship, hopefully friendly, found the lost ship. Admittedly, the chance was small, but it was a chance. The chambers, or pods, had their own power generators and could keep a person in stasis practically forever.

And that was the problem. Forever is a long time. The girls kissed me before we sealed ourselves into the pods. It seemed I had barely closed my eyes when the ringing of the ship's alarm awakened me. The lid to my pod was already open.

*Danger…Danger…Danger…*blared the speakers.

The first thing I was aware of, when I emerged from my coffin, was the cold. It was freezing in the control room. I was naked, and my body covered with goose bumps.

"Why is it so cold in here?" It was Sharina who climbed out of her pod, as naked as I.

Kabrina joined us a few moments later. "What's happened?" she asked, and rushed to the comm-center.

Danger…Danger…Danger…

"Can someone shut that damn thing off!" I yelled. Punching a few buttons on the control console, I overrode the ship's automatic system and put it into manual control. "Status?" I addressed the computer.

"*Warp jump aborted.*"

Dealing with computers can be frustrating. I had already figured out that we were back in normal space. I wanted to know why. The ship's screen showed nothing but empty space. If we had arrived there should have been a planet hanging there.

"Why was warp jump aborted?" I asked.

"*Capacitor failure.*"

"What?"

"*Capacitor failure.*"

"How in hell can the capacitors fail? We had everything checked out on Srax."

"*A detailed system's analysis can be printed out on request.*" The computer spoke with its pleasant female voice.

"Looks like the capacitors have been fried," Kabrina said.

"Accident?" I asked.

"No way to tell--just yet."

"Can you give us some heat? I'm freezing."

"I'm working on it." Sharina looked up from her console. "The computer sustained some damage when the capacitors broke down. For some unknown reason it began to shut down all life-support when we fell out of warped space. But I can override."

"Good. Kabrina, can you tell me where we are?"

"I have a fix on a system about 18 billion kilometers away."

I was afraid to ask the next question.

"Computer. Are we dead in space or do we still have sub-light capabilities?"

"*Please specify.*"

"How long until we reach the next planetary system?"

"*Nineteen days, five hours...*"

"Close enough." I sighed, somewhat relieved. "Computer. Is the system in the charts?"

"*System not in the charts, but it is known.*"

"Known? Explain."

"*System is the same as co-ordinates for target system.*"

I grinned at the girls. "Well, not all is lost. We have nineteen days to relax."

Chapter Seventeen

When we were seven days away from our destination, we began picking up radio signals. Our computer analyzed the language, and after 24 hours we had enough information in the databanks to decipher words and sentences. By the time we reached the outer planet, we had a fairly good command of the spoken language.

They came out of nowhere.

Two black delta-shaped spaceships streaked toward us shortly after we had passed the third planet. Again, there was no visual, just a harsh voice commanding us to leave immediately.

I didn't know if they would recognize my voice, but I wasn't taking any chances, so I let Kabrina handle the communication.

"This is Starsurfer," she said. "We are a trading vessel. Our jump-capacitors have been damaged beyond repair. We are lost and in need of assistance."

They didn't answer immediately. The silence and the two big black ships hanging threateningly on the screen were unnerving.

"They are scanning us," Sharina said from her console.

"Starsurfer prepare to be boarded."

All three of us let out a sigh of relief. At least they hadn't blown us out of space. Things were beginning to look up. Sharina opened the airlock. Watching our screen, we saw a small oval vessel detach itself from one of the big ships. About fifteen minutes later the computer reported that an object had attached itself to our ship. I took the elevator to the second level, walked down the corridor to the airlock.

Time to meet our guests. I was somewhat apprehensive. I knew this meeting wouldn't be as jovial as the one with Flightleader Horax of the Fifth Family. They entered the ship with weapons drawn, three big, black-clad soldiers with grim expressions and cold eyes.

"Identify yourself," the first one said, his long-barreled weapon pointing at me.

"I am Thomas Stone," I said, giving him my most disarming smile. "No need for weapons on my ship. None of us is armed."

"How many on your ship?" he asked. The barrel of his rifle had not moved.

"Just the three of us, but you know that already."

He gave me a cold stare. "Answer only what I ask!"

I had to suppress a smile. There would be no problem getting along with these people. They danced the same way we did. It was one of the first things they had taught me when I joined Special Forces. The Dance of Intimidation.

When you walk into a room filled with hostile people you don't walk in with your tail tucked between your legs. You attack. You intimidate. You act superior. You are superior! I could almost hear my instructor's voice shouting inside my head.

He strutted past me, headed for the stairs. His two companions followed without looking at me. They could have taken the elevator up, but I let them climb the narrow staircase. This way they had to pass the lounge where I had told Sharina and Kabrina to go.

As expected, both girls had changed into outfits that were more comfortable. Actually, I would have preferred them to be not quite as comfortable. Sharina was practically naked. I didn't even know she owned such a sheer outfit. And Kabrina had thrown a thin scarf around her hips; another narrow band of cloth covered her breasts.

They smiled sweetly when the three soldiers walked in.

"I am Sharina, and that is Kabrina, my sister." She held out a glass filled with red wine. "Can I offer you a welcome drink?"

"We are just so happy to see you," Kabrina chimed in. "We thought we'd surely die out there in the loneliness of space."

"Tell your companions to cover their bodies!" the leader of the three said harshly, looking at me.

I shrugged. "I am in no position to tell them anything." Grinning, I winked at him. "You know how women are. Sometimes it is best to humor them."

He glared at me. "I don't know how it is on your world. On mine, a woman is not the master of a man. If you want our assistance you'd be wise to remember that."

"Of course, of course," I said. "I'll make sure they behave themselves."

"Show my engineer the damage your ship has sustained."

One of his soldiers accompanied me to the power station, while he and the other one stayed with the girls.

"What system is this?" I tried to make conversation with the soldier. "We are totally lost. No idea where we are."

He glanced at me. "Then it is best it stays that way. Our world is closed to outsiders."

"I didn't know." I chuckled. "How could I? After all, we are lost. I hope the reason is not some kind of plaque, or is it? Are we in danger?"

"The only danger you are in is that I might have to close your mouth with the butt of my weapon," he snarled.

"Just trying to be friendly," I said.

We had arrived in the power station.

"Show me the damage," he demanded.

I pointed to the bank of capacitors. He walked around them, touched them, put his ear against one. Then he pulled a flat plate from his pocket, ran it over the capacitors, studied a small screen which he held in his hand. Shoving everything back into his pocked, he nodded, and then we marched back to the lounge.

"It is as we were told, the capacitors are dead," he said to the soldier in charge.

The leader nodded, gave me a hard stare. "We have a repair facility on one of the satellites. You will be directed there. And tell your females to put on some decent clothing, otherwise they will not be allowed to leave the repair facility."

With that, he turned and marched down the corridor, back to the airlock, followed by his two companions.

"I guess your little game of seduction failed," I said to the girls, after the soldiers were gone.

Sharina pouted. "That was the first time a male did pay me no attention. Maybe they were females in disguise."

I laughed and headed for the control room.

"Starsurfer. Be ready for transmission of co-ordinates, then proceed to your destination." The voice from the comm was harsh, cold.

Our computer acknowledged the downloading of the transmitted data, and soon we were on our way. It took over five hours to get to the satellite. We watched it appear on our screen. The round ball became a flat piece of landscape; it looked like any other moon I had seen, its craggy surface dotted with small and large craters, crevices, and deep canyons. After flying over a stretch of high mountains, our ship began to slow down. There was a large, flat area ahead of us; huge transparent bubbles covered it like mushrooms in a meadow after a rain. We landed beside one of these bubbles. Before our screen went black, I noticed that our ship was not the only ship on the landing pad. I counted five other vessels, all of them larger than ours, all of them armed. There was no mistaking the turrets for what they were, even though the sleek design of the craft partially concealed them. This place looked more like a military base than a colony of private citizens.

"Now what?" asked Sharina.

"I guess we wait." I said and shrugged.

It wasn't long before our screen sprang back to life. An official looking figure in a black uniform glared down at us. "Starsurfer. Do not attempt to leave your ship. We'll send a vehicle to pick you up."

"Understood." I said. "We'll be waiting."

The screen went dark again.

"I guess, we've been announced." I grinned at the girls. "They probably know everything about us by now." I looked them over. They had put on loose, gray robes that hid the shape of their bodies. I wore my tight, black pants, my spare black shirt, and a black cape. I figured I might as well make a good impression, since black seemed to be the color of choice here.

My head was bare. I hated that black skullcap.

"We should go, meet our welcoming committee," I said.

Each of the girls grabbed a small leather bag, which she carried over her shoulder. Then we went down to the airlock. We didn't have to wait long. The outer door to our ship opened, the inner door slid into its concealed envelope. Two black-clad men stood in the doorway. They had weapons, but they were holstered.

"Follow me," one of them said and turned to walk back through the short tunnel. The other one stayed behind, watched us enter the tunnel and then followed us. I turned to make sure the airlock sealed off our ship. But my concern was unfounded. These guys were on top of everything.

We boarded a small vehicle and I sank into a nice, soft seat, made myself comfortable. We didn't have a direct view to the outside. A large screen in the front displayed our surroundings. When our vehicle started to move it didn't head for the large bubble, which we had seen on our ship's screen, instead it passed it by and drove toward the mountains. The vehicle was not much different from the ones used by the colonies and Terran Forces on airless moons or on planets with a poisonous atmosphere. There were only the two guards who had welcomed us, and the driver of the vehicle. I guess the level of threat we might represent had been downgraded.

As our vehicle approached the flat wall in the face of the mountain, an opening suddenly appeared and we entered a short tunnel. Another opening and another tunnel. This one larger than the other one. After two more entry doors we finally ended up in some kind of hangar. Vehicles of all types and sizes were parked in several rows. The exit door to our vehicle opened and we were told to get out. Our guards delivered us to another, smaller vehicle. This time there were no guards, just the driver. I sat in front with the driver, the girls climbed into the back. There was no canopy, but the air inside the hangar was warm and surprisingly fresh smelling. Our new transportation took off the moment we were seated. The driver was a young man dressed in gray work-coveralls.

When we were out of sight of the guards, he turned to look at me. He actually smiled. "I am Hortas," he said. "You must be important people. I am supposed to take you to the Department of Defense."

I smiled back at him. "I am Thomas, and those two lovely creatures behind us are Sharina and Kabrina."

He threw the girls a quick glance. "You must indeed be important if they are allowed to go in public without their face-coverings."

"We are strangers here," I said. "Not quite familiar with your customs."

"They are not human, I can see that. Their eyes are strange." He gave me a quick look. "Are you human?"

I nodded, smiled. "There are people who question it, but I think I am."

"You must come from the Outside, from Forbidden Space. How did you get past the Defense Force?"

"Our ship broke down. We just drifted in, so to speak."

"Just the three of you?"

"That's right."

"What were you doing jumping around in space? What was your destination?"

"No particular place. We are merchants, looking for planets we can do business with." I grinned at him. "You are quite a curious young man."

He grinned back. "So I am."

"I am a little curious myself. We have no idea where this system of yours is located. Where in hell are we?"

"Nowhere in hell, I can assure you." He chuckled, "maybe close to it, though." He gave me a thoughtful look. "We have no contact with the rest of the Galaxy. That doesn't mean that we are ignorant of the existence of other worlds. We just don't allow outsiders on our world."

"Why not? What are you hiding that is so important?"

"What makes you think we are hiding something?" He spoke sharply, caught himself and laughed. "We are hiding nothing. It is just...the way we live...I mean, we don't want our way of life changed. Contact with other cultures may bring new beliefs and customs, not necessarily desirable."

"Sometimes change is good," I said. "It can be exciting and it brings progress. A culture that stagnates will die."

We had been driving inside a tunnel. There wasn't much traffic. Once in awhile another vehicle would come toward us, pass without slowing down. The tunnel ended suddenly and we shot into another huge cavern.

I was surprised to see the rows of houses on either side of the roadway. A number of miniature suns suspended from the high ceiling illuminated the whole cavern. They were bright enough to give the illusion of being on the surface of a planet.

We stopped in front of an official looking building complex. A couple of guards with weapons came down the steps, headed for our vehicle.

"This is where I must leave you," Hortas said. "Good luck."

"Thank you. Nice talking to you," I said and got out. One of the guards came up to me. "I'll have to search you for weapons."

"They are not dangerous," Hortas told him.

"I have my orders, sir." The guard frisked me, missed the knife in my boot. He was young. I was probably the first *dangerous* individual he's ever met. When he looked at the girls, Hortas laughed. "They're women. How dangerous can they be?"

The guard hesitated, and then shrugged. "I'm satisfied. Thank you, Captain."

I looked at Hortas. "Captain?"

He grinned, lifted his shoulders and drove off.

"In there," said the guard, indicating the large entrance door at the top of the stairs. We climbed up the stairs and entered the building.

Chapter Eighteen

We were escorted down a short corridor. There was a door at the end; it opened as we approached. A room full of desks. Through another door, this one thick and heavy, the room sparsely furnished. The man behind the massive desk gave us a hard look. After dismissing the two guards, he told us to sit down.

The chairs were as hard and cold as the man's eyes.

"So, you are the stranded merchants," he said while looking at a screen floating above his desk. "Nice ship. You must be doing well."

"We're doing alright. Haven't been too lucky, lately." I smiled.

He didn't. "Why are you here?"

I didn't think his already cold eyes could get any colder, but I was wrong. "You must have that information already," I said, patiently.

"Tell me again."

"Our ship broke down. This is the closest star system within reach." I leaned forward. "We wouldn't mind finding out where exactly we are, but everybody is so damn secretive."

"Are you spies?"

"We are merchants, not spies."

"You are from the human sector. The color of your ship, it betrays you. You are pirates."

I chuckled. "We've never robbed anyone. It just so happens I bought my ship from a dealer who may or may not have connections to pirates."

He gave me a calculating look. "No need to fabricate any stories. Those colors probably saved your life."

"Why? Do you prefer trading with pirates?"

He didn't answer my question. "For a simple merchant you are overly inquisitive," he said.

"It's one of my faults, I admit. Let me ask you another question: why don't we know anything about you, but you seem to know much about us? Why the secrecy?"

"Captain Horkas explained it to you. You should be satisfied with that."

"You've listened in on our conversation?"

"Not much happens without my knowledge. Let me give you some advice: watch what you say, wherever you are on our planet. Be careful whom you talk with. Do not speak to anyone about your origin. Do not stick you nose into things that are not your affair. Am I understood?"

"You made it very clear, sir. Another question: will my ship be repaired?"

"It will be. One problem though—the matter of payment."

"We have purple diamonds," Kabrina said.

He gave her a sharp look. "I don't remember speaking to you."

"She is a little eager sometimes," I said. "You have to forgive her." I could almost feel the daggers flying from her eyes, but I ignored her. This was no time to discuss a woman's pride or capabilities.

"You will be provided with appropriate clothing so your companions can appear in public. Once down on the planet you may find different conditions. Back to the matter of payment. I am giving you an opportunity to work off your debt."

"Work off my debt?" I echoed.

"It may take some time, depending how productive you are." His cold eyes stared into mine. "I am arranging for your ID chips and work permits. I hope you will not repay our generosity by creating problems."

"We'll try our best. Thank you for your trouble."

A black-clad guard took us to another room where a clerk pressed a tiny ID chip into our earlobes. The clerk was the first female we met. "Here are your work permits," she said through her black facemask and gave us three plastic cards. "Keep them in a safe place," she added, her voice low, as if afraid someone might overhear. Then she gave each of the girls a cape and a scarf and said, "You must cover your face at all times. And your bodies. It is the law."

The guard who had brought us was watching from the door. When we were done, he told us to follow him. He took us down an elevator. We ended up in a large room. As soon as we entered it, I felt a strange pulling inside my head; the darkness hidden inside my subconscious flared up briefly, but was gone moments later.

One wall of the room glimmered brightly. It was impossible to look at it for a long time without becoming nauseous.

"A portal," whispered Sharina beside me.

"Let's go!" the guard barked. "Step through!"

"Through what?" I asked.

"The gate. Step through the gate." He stood in front of the shimmering wall.

Sharina was the first one to approach the wall. She hesitated for a moment, and then she walked into it and disappeared. No flash. No thunder. Nothing. She was just gone. Kabrina was the next to go. The guard stared at me. I shrugged and followed the girls. It was like stepping through a door. The room I stepped into was bigger than the one I had left. Bright lights flooded through a large window. There was a desk, behind it another black-clad official. Sharina and Kabrina were standing in front of the desk. When the official saw me, he waved me over.

"Name and status?" he asked.

I handed him my work permit and said, "Thomas Stone."

The official eyed me, curiosity plainly showing in his face. "This permit was signed by the High Commissioner of Security himself. You must be people of great importance."

I shrugged, grinned. "I guess we are."

Scanning his screen, he said, "You are instructed to wait for someone to pick you up. Do not leave this building." He pointed. "Go through that door."

We walked into another large room. It had chairs and benches, obviously some kind of waiting room. There was nobody else present. In one corner I saw a blinking eye, probably a surveillance camera or some other spying device. The girls had seen it, too. They looked at me, but said nothing. Sharina sat down, pulled up her cape to expose her legs. "This is ridiculous," she said. Her face was hidden behind the scarf, only her emerald eyes were visible. They flashed angrily.

We waited about an hour, when finally an older man walked through the door. "I am Sevare," he said. "I will take you to your place of employment."

An elevator took us down to ground level. We boarded a sleek vehicle that rose into the air as soon as we were seated. Skimming the rooftops of high-rising buildings I got an excellent bird's eye view of the city and realized it was not very big.

We left the city behind and headed west.

Sevare put the skimmer on automatic pilot and swiveled his chair to face us. "I guess you are wondering where we are going?"

"A little," I admitted. "But does it really matter?"

"Probably not." Looking at the girls, he said, "I know you've been told to veil your faces. This vehicle is not connected to the government sensor net. Feel free to relax."

"Thank you." Sharina unwrapped her veil, opened her cape and robe. Kabrina did the same. Sevare lifted his eyebrows slightly when he saw them in their tight-fitting bodysuits. "Maybe you shouldn't relax too much," he commented dryly. "We are not used to seeing our women this revealed, except in our ceremonies."

Below us, I saw cultivated fields and vast areas of grass-covered prairie. "Those herds," I said, "are they some kind of food animal?"

"We call them Cerebs. And you are correct, they are food animals."

"Meat is an essential food?"

"For some. Others prefer to eat only vegetable matter."

"Things are not much different here from other planets," Kabrina commented.

Sevare smiled. "Why should they be?"

"How much were you told about us?" I asked.

"I know you are from the Outside. Not much else."

"We are supposed to work off a debt. How? I don't know. What will I be doing?"

"My employer provides agricultural services. Do you know how to fly an aircraft?"

"I am trained as a pilot."

"Then that's what you'll most likely be doing. Spraying crops. We are always looking for pilots."

"How about us?" Kabrina asked.

He looked her over. "You might be employable as a courtesan. It is obvious that you like to display your body."

Sharina hissed loudly and looked at her sister. "And here we thought these people are far advanced. I guess we were wrong."

"Whatever customs you're used to, forget them." Sevare warned. "For your own well-being you must learn to keep your thoughts to yourself. It is very important that you know your place. You may not agree with our ways, but that is how we live, and you are strangers here. Never forget that."

His eyes fastened on me. "I don't know your relationship with these two females, and I don't need to know. They are your responsibility. Take my advice, keep them in line." He turned back to his controls.

Kabrina looked at me. Her emerald eyes sparkled mischievously. "Are you up to the task, Thomas?" she asked, giving me an innocent smile. Somehow, I didn't see the humor. "Just don't give me any trouble," I murmured. Of course, I knew it was like asking a fox not to eat the chickens. These two females were trouble incarnate.

We skirted another, smaller city, flew over more fields, large forests, and even larger prairies. The land was flat, but in the far distance I caught glimpses of mountains, their peaks shrouded by hazy clouds.

"How large is the population on your planet?" I asked.

Sevare gave me a quick glance. "On this continent around sixteen million."

"There are more continents?"

"One more, smaller than this one. We are not exactly on friendly terms, which means, we don't exchange information. If I were to guess, I'd say there are approximately ten million people living there."

"A small population for such a large planet."

"We like it that way."

"No commerce with other planets?"

He looked at me for moment, shrugged. "I was told not give you too much information. No reason given. So let us end the questions here."

I smiled. "There it is again."

"What?"

"The secrecy. What are you people hiding?"

"I am not aware of anything we might want to hide. But it would be wise not to ask so many questions." Sevare smiled. "Maybe we are just a secretive race." He turned back to his consol, touched some controls. "We'll be landing in a few minutes."

There were buildings ahead. I saw a number of aircraft parked in front of what could only be a hangar.

Our craft settled down gently beside one of the others.

"Welcome to the Collingdale Estate." Sevare rose from his seat.

The door slid open and I was the first to get off. A small cloud of dust rose when I jumped to the ground.

"It's the dry season," Sevare remarked behind me. "It can become quite dusty."

Sharina crinkled her nose. "What's that smell?" she asked.

"There is a Cereb ranch to the west of us, and when the wind blows from the right direction our noses have to suffer a little." He saw me study the other aircraft. They were not sleek and streamlined, like the one we had arrived in, but more boxier and larger. "Those are the Sprayers," Sevare explained. "You'll most likely be flying one of them."

"I know how to fly a Floater," Kabrina said.

"Our females don't fly aircraft," Sevare said, "not usually, anyway.

He looked disapprovingly at her and Sharina. "Please, cover your face. Some of our employees are stout *Believers*. It wouldn't be good to have them see you like this."

Both girls pouted, but complied with his request. "This is going to be difficult," Sharina complained. "I'm used to having males look at me."

"I'm sure, you are. Maybe we can find you an appropriate occupation," Sevare said dryly.

Out of one of the buildings strode a figure dressed in a loose, flowing robe. A female, judging by the veiled face and long black hair, which she had tied loosely to one side of her face. It hung down almost to her hip.

Approaching us, she stopped in front of me. She had lovely dark eyes with long thick lashes. "So, you are our new pilot?" Her voice was soft and pleasant. And young.

I smiled at her. "I am Thomas Stone. And you?"

"This is Skyla." Sevare answered for her. "She is our employer's granddaughter."

I detected disapproval in his voice.

"I can speak for myself," Skyla said, still looking at me. "Sevare believes that a female's place is in the house, away from all the action."

"Your criticism is misplaced, my lady. I am only concerned with your safety."

Skyla laughed. *If she is as beautiful as her laugh,* I thought, *I'm looking forward to seeing her without her robe and veil.*

"I am not a little child, Sevare, not anymore," she said and looked at Sharina and Kabrina. "Are you his mates?"

"We belong to no one," Sharina answered.

Was that jealousy I detected in her voice? Funny, how women always seem to perceive a rival in another woman.

"They are my companions," I said, "my team mates."

"I will introduce you to your employer," Sevare broke in and turned to Skyla. "Take these two to their quarters and give them a few lessons in etiquette. They are strangers to our world."

Chapter Nineteen

He was an imposing figure. Big and massive. His face lined, stern. It was hard to judge his age, but he was way past middle age.

"I am Sir John Collingdale the Third." His voice was deep, resonant.

"Sir John Collingdale?" I repeated. My expression must have betrayed me.

"A title that has been handed down in our family for generations. We can trace our roots back to the time when our ancestors first set foot on this planet." He smiled. "I am human. In case you are wondering."

"Isn't everyone on your planet?" I asked.

"There were people living here when humans arrived. They looked like us, but they were not human."

"Where are they now?"

"Still here."

"What makes them different?"

"There really is no difference." He shrugged. "The color of their eyes, mainly. Crossbreeding is possible, and it happens frequently. But we keep records. There are many fractions on either side that are against interracial marriages."

"I guess discrimination is well and alive on every planet," I said.

"I don't know about other planets," he said. "Only certain government officials are allowed access to that kind of information."

"But you are not ignorant of the fact that there are other populated worlds, are you?"

"Our government tries to keep us isolated. We are not allowed travel to the Outside, but there are reasons for that."

"And you are aware of those reasons?"

He chuckled. "We don't question the reasons of the Guardian Council. At least we're not supposed to." He studied me with narrow eyes. "According to my information, you are a merchant whose ship broke down. It left you stranded in our system. It also says you are a pilot. Somehow I get the impression there is more to you than what I'm told."

"I seem to give that impression." I smiled at him.

He kept looking at me. "I have no interest in politics. I keep my opinions to myself. I don't make trouble and I don't look for trouble. I hope you live by the same code."

"I'm not looking for trouble, either," I said. I failed to mention that I was a favorite of the *Gods of Trouble*.

"What about your two companions?"

I lifted my shoulders and spread my hands. "Who knows? They are females. Not even human. Strangers. I admit they have given me some cause for concern, sometimes. But I'm sure they will behave, as long as we are here."

"That may be a long time." He didn't smile when he said that.

"How long?"

"I don't know." He cleared his throat. "As I told you, I stay away from politics. You must be tired. Get a good night's rest. Tomorrow you will familiarize yourself with your work. The sooner you are ready to begin, the better. We have an extremely dry season this year, and the Seedjumpers are breeding fiercely. Crops are being destroyed at an alarming rate, and there is a shortage of qualified crop-dusters. It is demanding work, and sometimes dangerous. Volunteers are rare." His expression was one of quiet amusement. "Fortunately for us, you have been volunteered. Few of our pilots are here by choice. Most of them are considered criminals."

Well, I should feel right at home here. After all, wasn't I one of them?

"Anything else I need to know?" I asked. My enthusiasm for this new job was not enhanced by his revelations.

"That is all for now." Smiling, he dismissed me.

* * * *

My quarters were comfortable. A nice bed in an air-conditioned room, a small mirror over a dresser, and a large window to watch the sunset. The washroom was down the hall. Obviously, there were others I had to share it with. I slept well that night. There were no dreams to disturb my rest. A knock on the door woke me up. When I looked out the window, I saw that the sun was just creeping into the sky. It was tempting to go back to sleep, but this was my first day on the job. It was best to make a good impression. I got dressed, went out into the hall and walked to the bathroom. When I opened the door, the sight of four naked men taking a shower greeted me.

"You must be the new flyer," one of them, a big, muscular guy said, grinning. "We usually take off our clothes before we shower."

I grinned back. "So do I." I began to strip. They watched me, and I saw their eyes widen when I was naked. Even the big fellow studied me with interest.

"What are you? Some kind of arena-fighter?"

"Just another pilot," I said.

"Those muscles. No normal man is built like that. You look like one of the statues of the Golden God." The speaker, a short skinny man with gray hair, stared at me. "You're no ordinary pilot. Where are you from?"

"From far away. Very far away."

"Are you from Arenia?"

I nodded and stepped into the shower.

"Are you some kind of spy?"

"That's it." I smiled through the spray of water. "I came here to find out how you people get rid of the Seedjumpers."

The others laughed. The skinny one didn't think it was funny. "A spy and a comedian." He spit out a mouthful of water. "Is everyone there built like you?"

"Pretty well." I grinned at him.

The big man laughed and handed me a bar of soap. "Don't mind Skarrol. He is kind of paranoid. Thinks Arenia is going to attack us any day now."

"They will. You just wait and see." Skarrol glared at him, then at me. "Remor may be as big as a cereb; he also has the brain of one. I know things."

One of the others left the shower, reached for a towel. "He's been breathing too much seed-jumper spray, that Skarrol. According to his theory, the outbreak of the Seedjumpers is the first wave of the attack. You coming here may just confirm that. By the way, I'm Arwin."

"I'm Thomas," I said. "Thomas Stone."

* * * *

The Flyers were easy to master. The controls were simple and even though the craft were boxy-looking, they skimmed through the air on silent wings. The problem was the damned spray equipment. It wasn't exactly state-of-the-art. *Can't afford it,* I was told. *The chemicals are so harsh, they eat the sprayers and tubes. Replacement parts are expensive.* On my first day I accompanied Arwin as a co-pilot. He explained everything quite well.

"Don't fly too high," he told me, "especially if you're near a lake or river. That stuff we're spraying is toxic. Wear your mask at all times. Don't trust the illusionary safety of the cabin. Fumes may get in somehow; by the time you smell them it is too late. They'll burn your lungs right out."

109

"No electronic detectors?"

He grimaced behind his mask. "What do you think?"

The fields we sprayed stretched for endless kilometers. Land was plentiful and apparently quite fertile.

We stopped for lunch when the sun was a burning ball high in the blue sky. Arwin sat the aircraft down beside a pristine looking lake. There were groves of tall trees to provide us with shade. We ate biscuits with smoked meat and some fruit. Lying on my back, looking into the cloudless sky, I remembered my new employer's words. *Most of them are considered criminals*. Arwin seemed like a descent fellow. I couldn't picture him doing something illegal.

"Why are you doing this kind of work?" I asked him.

"Why are *you* doing this kind of work?" he countered.

"I'm paying off a debt."

He sat up and looked down at me. "You're not really from Arenia, are you?"

I considered his question for a moment. It may be time for some truth. "Not really," I said. "I come from much farther away."

"You're from off-planet. From one of the colonies. Why did they send you back?"

"I wasn't aware that you have colonies," I said.

His eyes widened a little. "Are you telling me that you are from the Outside?"

"What if I am?"

"It would confirm our suspicions. You see, our leaders tell us that no ordinary human can cross the energy barrier that isolates us from the rest of the Galaxy. The ones who try and succeed end up going insane. Only the *Chosen*, the ones blessed by the Guardian Council, can overcome the onslaught of visions and nightmare images that assault the senses when traveling through warped space. Yet--here you are, claiming to be from the *Outside*, apparently quite sane."

"I assure you, I am sane. It is true about the visions--they can be traumatic. They may leave you a little troubled for awhile, but they won't drive you insane."

"How did you get here?"

"In a spaceship." I smiled. "Why? Is there another way?"

His eyes avoided mine. "I wouldn't know what you are talking about. You say you are working off a debt?"

"My ship broke down. I'm having it repaired."

"You'll never be able to pay it off, you know that?" His eyes were grave.

I picked a blade of grass, stuck it into my mouth, sucked on it. It tasted bitter. As bitter as the news I was going to get. He was going to confirm what had been gnawing in my guts for some time now. "Is it because this job pays so little?" I asked, fully knowing it was the wrong question.

He shook his head. "Because you'll never be allowed to leave here."

"Why not?"

"You don't know the history of our planet, do you?"

"I know nothing about your planet. Not even its name."

"*Hellsgate*, that's what we humans call it. The official name is *Ramarra*. It is an ancient word and means *Portal*."

"The portal to what?"

He grinned, shrugged. "Hell."

"Interesting." I watched a flock of small birds circling one of the trees, then take refuge among the thick branches. Listening to their happy, musical songs I felt relaxed and at peace. "This seems like a peaceful planet," I said.

"It could be, if it weren't for the snakes in the grass." He chuckled when I bolted upright. "Figuratively speaking, I mean."

"No snakes?"

"No snakes. Not here, anyway." He became serious. "This is an old planet. There were others here long before us, even before the *Ra-el-marras* settled here."

"Ra-el-marras? You're talking about the people who were here when the humans came?"

"That's right. Ra-el-marras is their word for *The-Ones-Who-Keep-Watch.*"

"When did humans arrive here?"

"About a thousand years ago. That is the old Standard Year. Our ancestors were colonists from Earth. Their destination lay apparently somewhere else, but because of a malfunction, the colony-ship dropped out of warped space. They had no choice but to settle on Ramarra. Even then this system was already closed to outsiders, and the humans were forbidden to leave again, or contact Earth."

"How many humans are living on Ramarra?"

Arwin shrugged. "I don't really have access to that kind of information. Maybe five million who are still pure blood."

"Any on the other continent, on Arenia?"

111

"No idea how many, but I think the majority of Arenians is human. Why the interest?"

I smiled. "If I'm stuck here I want to know as much as I can. Knowledge is power, you know."

"Too much knowledge is dangerous. Be careful. The Guardian Watchers are everywhere. I might be one of them." He grinned.

"Are you?"

"No."

"You've never told me why you are here."

He stood up, stretched. "Time to get back to work. Did you know that Adam and Eve were thrown out of Paradise because they thirsted for knowledge?"

"I know the story," I said. "It was the serpent who seduced Eve."

"Satan. He's the reason humans lost Paradise. We've been searching ever since to find the gates again."

I had to grin. "Seems you've found the gates on Ramarra."

"The gates to Hell."

"Or Paradise, who knows."

"Who knows." He began walking toward our aircraft. "Come, let's go."

The birds took flight, protesting loudly when we approached their hiding place. I watched the flock disappear into the trees on the other side of the lake.

Lucky little creatures. Were they searching for a paradise lost? Probably not. They had already found it on the other side of the lake.

As we rose into the sky, I searched out their tree. One sweep of the Sprayer would wipe out the whole flock. Even in paradise, there was no safety, but they didn't know it. They were blessed in their ignorance.

Underneath us rolled the mass of grain fields filled with golden seeds. We didn't see the Seedjumpers, but Arwin assured me they were there. Working the buttons that activated the sprayers, we sent death to an army of unseen tiny creatures who had been as ignorant as the birds. They had felt safe in their golden paradise, until the gates of Hell opened above them to bring the knowledge of death--if only for a short moment.

Chapter Twenty

I hadn't seen the girls for days. When I asked Remor, who turned out to be our supervisor, I was told that they had been taken to another site, where they were taught to fly a Sprayer. *We need every able pilot, and they apparently are quite capable.*

On the fourth day I was on my own. They gave me a co-pilot: a short, fat, balding guy, who had never flown anything in his life. But he was quite good when it came to operating the spraying equipment. His name was Crollin. He didn't talk much, which suited me just fine. It took all my skills to maneuver the aircraft, an old model that had seen better days.

On our third day it broke down.

We were just flying over the ruins of an old, abandoned city, when lights began flashing all over my screen.

Emergency landing sequence initiated... Emergency landing sequecence initiated... crackled the speakers.

The controls didn't respond. All we could do was to strap in and hope for the best. We skimmed the old ruins much too close for comfort and finally came to rest just outside the city. When I radioed for help I was told to sit tight, someone would come and pick us up in the morning.

"Looks like we'll spend the night."

Crollin wasn't overly exited, and neither was I. The Sprayers weren't meant for sleeping. We had just barely enough room to swivel our chairs around and stretch our legs.

"Maybe we'll find some shelter in those ruins," I said.

Crollin shook his head. "Not me. I'm not going in there."

"Why not?"

"That place is haunted. All the old cities are."

"Nonsense. I don't believe in ghosts."

"Not ghosts. *Makkala.* The Lost Ones. They drink your blood. Steal your soul. When you sleep."

"Still nonsense. Creatures that drink blood are flesh and bone. They can be killed."

"They are already dead. I'm not going into the city, and I advise you not to." He had become quite agitated. These Makkala must scare the hell out of him; he hadn't talked this much for the last three days. It is funny how superstition and religion can make babbling idiots out of usually rational people.

We finished eating our rations. Crollin made himself comfortable underneath the Sprayer. I was restless. The old city seemed to pull me as a magnet pulls a lump of iron. There were still at least three hours of daylight left, so I decided to go exploring.

Collin seemed frantic when I told him, but he resigned to the fact that I was his boss. "It's your soul," he said. I could see the beads of perspiration on his forehead, even though the evening was cool.

"Don't worry," I told him. "I'll be back before dark."

The city was old, older than anything I had ever seen. Professor Elisa Stone, my adopted mother, had shown me holograms of ancient cities on other planets. The architecture of these buildings was different from any of the ruins of the vanished ancient civilizations she had found. Could she be here, she'd be ecstatic.

Even though incredibly old, some of the buildings were still wonderfully preserved. Wind and rain had left their mark on the natural stone, but they had also kept the walls clean of vines and moss.

Looking at the buildings, it was hard to believe that nobody lived here. The glass in the windows was scoured and scratched, but unbroken. Thick dust and dirt covered the roads, but when I bent down to scratch the surface, I exposed a shiny, glass-like substance.

It was eerily silent. I didn't even hear any birds, or other animals.

When I entered one of the buildings, I found the rooms empty of furnishings. There was nothing but piles of dust and scraps of rusted metal. It was comforting to know that the ancients had not been perfect after all; it seems not all materials they had used endured the passage of time.

I kept to the main road. Didn't feel like getting lost in some back-lane, not at this time of day. Most buildings were two and three stories high. There were no high-risers.

The road ended in a large courtyard. On the other side rose a majestic structure. Thick round pillars framed a huge gate, which led into the interior. Elaborately carved statues stood on ledges, and some were etched right into the stone. On either side of the gate, the golden statues of two muscular winged men guarded the entrance to the building.

When I walked past them, a shiver ran through my body, as if some electric current had touched my skin.

The men carried swords in their hands. Inside, more statues. Of men and women. Some nude, some dressed in long, flowing robes.

Some with wings and some without. All the women were beautiful, the men handsome and muscular.

I was just admiring the lifelike statue of a winged woman when I heard a scrabbling noise behind me.

When I whirled around, I saw something running past me. I couldn't make out what it was, since it moved with incredible speed. All I saw was a dark shape, the size of a large dog. Two more raced past. I bent to pull the knife out of my boot, held it in front of me.

More and more came, began surrounding me. Some took to the air, landed on top of ledges, where they crouched on powerful hind legs.

They had flat, ugly faces. Their powerful jaws revealed long canines; their red eyes stared at me from inside deep sockets. I noticed that they had black bat-like wings, and human hands, with long bony fingers, tipped with sharp claws.

"What do you seek, human?"

I hadn't heard her come in. She suddenly stood in front of me.

Her skin was pure white, her face a beautiful vision, her eyes large and deep green. Her hair was long and straight, and as white as her skin. She was completely naked. Between her legs, her pubis was thick and hairless. Her labia glowed with a soft purple hue.

From her shoulders sprouted a pair of giant wings, like the wings of a butterfly, splashed with the colors of the rainbow.

Behind her full red lips I could see white even teeth. I also saw two small, pointy fangs. "What do you seek, human?" she asked, again.

"Knowledge," I said. "I was curious."

She smiled. "There is nothing to be learned in this place. No one lives here."

"Except you."

"No one lives here," she repeated. "The glory of this once great city has not been spoken of for a long time. You are foolish to come here." She stared at me with her green eyes. "Any who trespass never leave again."

"Are you going to stop me?"

"Not I. They will." She pointed at the horde of squatting creatures, who sat unmoving all around me, watching me with red glowing eyes.

"Who are you?" I asked.

"I am Makkala. Don't you know?"

I shrugged. "Not really. Until today I've never heard of the Makkala, the Lost Ones."

She laughed. "We are not lost. The humans call us that."

"You said you don't live here. Where do you live?"

"I do not live. I exist."

"Where do you exist?"

"Not where. When."

"You speak in riddles. Tell me then: when do you exist?"

"Forever."

"You are an immortal?"

She came closer, stood in front in me. Her eyes bored into mine. "You are very curious. Her hand reached out, touched my face. "Do you seek pleasure, human?"

The touch of her hand was like a small electric shock. "Are you offering yourself?" I asked. Putting a hand on her breast, I squeezed it gently. She felt warm and soft. Whatever she was or pretended to be, her body was real--and inviting.

She pulled away, laughing. Her great wings moved with sudden fury. She rose into the air. There was a giant statue of a golden man with half-spread wings. She circled around it, and then settled on top of his head, perched on small feet and hands. Her wings moved gently, keeping her balanced.

"Take off your clothes," she called down to me.

I looked at the silent watchers. They squatted like statues, motionless; only their eyes seemed alive. "They won't harm you," she said. "Unless I tell them to."

I took off my boots, laid my knife beside them, within easy reach. Then I removed the rest of my clothing.

She launched herself into the air again, landed on light feet in front of me. Her hands stroked my biceps, my chest. Again I felt the tingle on my skin. Soft fingers circled around my penis and squeezed it gently. She laughed when it grew hard in the sheath of her hand. "You desire me?" she asked softly.

"You are beautiful," I said and put my hand between her legs. Her slit was slippery to my touch. I pushed my finger inside her. Putting her slim arms around my neck, she lifted up and kissed me with open lips. When I pushed my tongue past her teeth, I tasted the sweetness of her mouth.

She broke the kiss, pushed me away. Then she lay down on the floor. Her wings spread beneath her like a soft, colorful blanked. They looked fragile, but I saw the strong, muscular ribbing that was inside the tough skin.

Her legs spread wide, her pink orifice beckoned. I knelt between her open thighs, let her hands guide my stiff member toward her sex-organ. "Don't be afraid," she whispered and smiled. "Only pleasure awaits you."

I slid into her creamy sheath with ease and felt soft walls mold around my hard organ. When I came inside her for the first time she wanted to push my off, but I held her down until I was finished.

"You are very strong," she murmured.

I put my hands under her buttocks and began to move forcefully on top of her, pushing deep with every stroke.

After my third climax she said, "Let me be on top. You must be tiring."

"Not really." I laughed, but pulled out of her. Lying on my back, I watched her hover over me. She kept herself afloat by slowly beating her wings. Very carefully, she settled into my lap, taking me deep inside her. Looking into my eyes, she began moving her wings up and down, working her inner muscles. Her body lifted a little, and then she sank back into my lap, sucking my penis back into her belly. She kept this up for a long time.

"Now!" she called out. "Release your sperm now."

I had been ready for a while, and pushing up I let go. She bent forward, collapsing her wings like a cloak on top of us. Her breasts were soft and warm on my chest. Kissing me fiercely, she milked my spurting organ with rhythmic pulsating of her tight sheath.

At the height of my orgasm I felt a ghostly finger touch my mind, probe.

Deep inside me, the darkness rose with a roar.

She cried out.

"It was a mistake," she stammered, sitting up. Her eyes were large, frightened. "Forgive me. I didn't know."

As quickly as it had risen the darkness subsided, but stayed watchful. I was aware of its presence.

I put my hands around her slim hips, held her imprisoned on top of me. My penis was still hard inside her warm vagina. "Whatever it was you just tried," I said softly, "don't try it again. It could be fatal."

She shook her head and stared at me. "How can I redeem myself?" she asked in a small voice.

"You can copulate with me until we both drop from exhaustion."

"That is impossible. I can go on forever."

"Well--then we have no problem. So can I."

We fucked long and hard, changing positions every so often. She had beautiful plump buttocks, round and firm. It was a pleasure to watch those lovely cheeks squeeze my shaft. I never noticed the passage of time. Outside, it was dark, but the bright disk of the moon was visible through the windows, bathing us with pale light.

Her attitude toward me changed. She acted aloof and superior before, now she was subdued and servile, eager to please. "Are you satisfied with the level of pleasure I am giving you?" she asked, as she gyrated her hips above me.

"You are an expert," I said, enjoying the soft pressure of her pulsating vagina walls around my penis.

"You must leave here soon," she said suddenly.

"Why?"

"Others are coming."

"Others?"

"Makkala. Ela-Makkala. They will not approve of my behavior. I will be challenged." Her green eyes reflected the moonlight, made them glow softly. She moved forward, her breasts grazed my skin. "You are *shakka*."

I took her nipple between my teeth, touched it with my tongue. She moaned softly. "You are awakening things in me which are forbidden," she whispered and began snapping her pelvis with fierce movements. "Come now! Give me the gift of life."

I exploded one last time, and then I pulled out of her. I was still stiff. She stood up, looked down at me. A smile played around her full lips. Her colorful wings folded behind her, like the wings of a butterfly. I closed my eyes for a moment. When I opened them, she was gone. So were her ugly companions.

Getting up, I looked for my clothes. It was suddenly dark inside the room. The moon had moved from its high position in the night sky. Bumping into a few statues, I managed to find my way out without injuring myself too much.

The night was silent. A brisk wind from the west cooled down my heated body. Slowly I began walking back the way I had come.

Chapter Twenty-one

The rescue plane came shortly after sunrise. I was surprised to see Skyla. She was dressed in a loose-fitting flyer-outfit. Her head was bare, her long black hair braided into a thick rope, but her face was veiled, and again I wondered what she looked like underneath.

The man with her was tall and thin, with a permanent frown on his narrow face. He climbed out, carrying a case filled with instruments and gauges. "I can't fix it here," he announced after examining our engine. "We'll have to bring the anti-grav lifters and tow it back into the repair shop."

"Well, I guess that means you'll have to come with us," Skyla said, looking at me.

I shrugged. "Whatever you say."

During the flight home Crollin kept throwing furtive glances at me. "Who are you?" he blurted out, suddenly.

"I am Thomas Stone. Who else would I be?"

He shook his head. "You look human. But are you?"

I laughed. "Doubts have been raised before."

"Any problems?" Skyla asked from the pilot's chair.

"He's been in the ancient city. All night," Crollin said with an accusing voice.

The girl turned away from her controls, gave me a long stare. "It is forbidden, you know."

"I didn't know."

"Did you see anything?"

"Plenty of ruins. Surprising how well some of the buildings are preserved. That city must be very old. I went inside a building that looked like a place of worship. Lots of statues of gods and goddesses."

"Anything else?"

"I met one of the Makkala and her minions. Ugly creatures."

Her eyes widened. She touched her forehead with the tip of two fingers. "The Makkala?" Her voice was almost a whisper. "You must be mistaken. What did she look like?"

"A beautiful woman with the wings of a butterfly."

"Did you talk to her?"

I smiled at her. "We talked."

"Nobody talks to the Makkala and lives. You were probably just dreaming. How do you know about the Lost-Ones?"

"They are not lost," I said.

"Who says?"

"She told me. She told me many things. We had…" I smiled. "Let's say we had an interesting conversation."

"If what you say is true you are not what you seem. No human has ever encountered one of the Makkala and lived. Only the High Priests of the Ra-el-marras are allowed in the ancient holy places. Only they have the power to resist the Makkala." Her eyes were thoughtful. I noticed that the dark iris of her eyes was flecked with tiny motes of gold. "Do you believe in the existence of the Golden God?" she asked me.

Lifting my shoulders, I chuckled. "I am not a member of that cult, if that's what you're asking."

"Choose your words carefully when you speak about the Believers," she warned me. "There are those who may find your views and attitude offensive."

"Do you?"

"I might."

"It wasn't my intention to offend you. I've never been a great believer in religion, any religion. But I don't belittle those who are. My apologies."

She didn't say anything, just kept looking at me. I wished I could see her expression. Was she smiling? Annoyed? Angry?

"I know all about you. My grandfather told me. You are a stranger here. It is not your fault," she said, finally. "I should apologize. Maybe a change in some of our beliefs would be an advantage. Our society has become stagnant. There is no progress. Our priests tell us things will change when the Golden God returns"

"But there are those who warn about those changes," Crollin broke in.

"The Gatekeepers. They say that the Golden God will bring chaos." Skyla sighed. "Whom do you believe?"

"I don't know if you are aware of this, probably not: the Golden God has quite a following on many worlds," I said. "On some worlds the cult is outlawed and its followers persecuted."

"I didn't know." Skyla sounded surprised. "On Ramarra the Believers are in the majority and no one would dare harm us. It is an old religion. Almost as old as that of the Gatekeepers."

"The Gatekeepers. What do they believe in?"

"According to the legends the Ra-el-marras, the *Ones-Who-Keep-*

Watch, were sent here by the Guardians to protect the Gates and to watch out for the return of *The-One-Who-Was-Outcast*. Not to welcome him, but to keep him from entering the Gates."

"The Gates to where?" I remembered asking Arwin the same question.

Skyla shrugged. "I don't know. Maybe the place where the ancient Guardians live now."

"Why would they want to keep the Golden God out?"

"You ask too many questions. I can't believe that you are that ignorant." She turned back to her controls. "Then again--maybe you are. This afternoon I have to fly to the city. If you truly are interested in my religion, you can accompany me there. It might be in your best interest to learn more about life on Ramarra."

Sir John Collingdale seemed to hesitate when Skyla asked for his permission to let me go with her to the city, but then he nodded and smiled. "If that's what you wish," he said and gave me a stern look. "My granddaughter's welfare is quite important to me. She is a very special individual, as you will find out. For reasons I cannot understand she seems to have taken a liking to you. Do nothing that might bring her harm. Understand?"

"I will protect her with my life," I said, and I meant it.

He smiled. "No need to become dramatic. I don't think you will get into any situations that involve life and death. Just promise me to stay an impartial observer, to hold your tongue and keep your opinions to yourself. And try not to draw too much attention to your person. The Guardians are watching, especially in the city."

We left after lunch. Skyla had changed her flyer outfit into a loose-fitting wraparound. Her long hair was hidden inside a hood. She told me to fly, since females in her position were not allowed to operate any craft.

"You were flying before," I said, puzzled.

"Outside of the cities we take some liberties," she said. "City-life is different."

The route to the city was programmed into the craft's navigation system. I really didn't have much to do, but sit in the pilot's seat. The aircraft was a sleek two-seater, nothing like the antiquated Sprayers. It was comfortable and built for speed, but Skyla told me to set the speed to low. There was no hurry.

"Tell me about the worlds Outside," she said.

"What do you want to know?"

"Your companions, Sharina and Kabrina, they are not human. Are there many non-human races?"

"Yes, there are."

"Tell me of some." She had thrown back her hood. She looked at me eagerly with her gold-flecked eyes.

"Well--there are the Korillians. Only recently, I spent some time on their planet. They are humanoid. Their faces are not ugly, if you like flat noses and bulging eyes. How they ever developed space travel is beyond me. They are not too bright.

Another species I've had contact with not so long ago are the Flemlins. Beautiful people. Highly advanced technologically. Quite fierce and warlike. Can be cruel and vicious.

I've also spent some time with the Srax. Of reptilian ancestry, they don't like humans, but we've had dealings with them. The ones I've met were no different from most humans. They live, love and hate, just like us.

Then we have the Vegans, also a reptilian race. Rude and loud. They don't have many friends.

The Kapellans are birdlike beings, with long, thin necks. As peaceful and gentle as they look, that's how ill-tempered they are.

I forgot to mention the Thorans. A race of assassins. I'm surprised they haven't killed off each other by now. If you want someone dead, you hire a Thoran. Usually they get the job done with great efficiency."

"So many different beings. So many different cultures and histories. Do they ever crossbreed? How are the offspring treated?"

"Not all are compatible, but, yes, many races mix. On some planets the offspring are accepted, on some they are not. On Eden's Gate, for instance, humans will mate with the Katr, who were the original inhabitants. Any children of those unions are considered subhuman and not treated well." I closed my eyes for a moment, remembering Renha. *I wonder what she is doing. And Rinca, her cousin. Did I really get them pregnant? How will my children be treated?*

"What do they all believe in?" Skyla's voice brought me back to the present.

Opening my eyes, I smiled at her. "They all believe in some kind of deity. Life on most planets is harsh. Any thinking creature inevitably will ask the question: what happens after I die? Is there an afterlife? Is it better than this one? That is really what religion is all about."

"There is more to religion than just believing in an afterlife. For some it is a way of life, a celebration of this life."

I shrugged. "As I told you before, I am not into religion. Believe anything you like, but allow me my own beliefs; and do not hate me because my beliefs are not yours. A truly religious person is not a fanatic, but tolerant of others. Love your friends and your enemies alike."

She put her hand on mine. It felt warm and soft. "I don't hate you because you are not one of the Believers," she said gently. Her fingers trembled suddenly. She pulled her hand away. "There is something about you," she whispered. "It attracts me to you. But it cannot happen. Must not happen. You are unlike anyone I've ever met."

"Do you ever take off your face covering?" I asked.

"When I eat. When I bathe or when I am alone, unobserved. It is allowed."

"Those are the only times?" When I looked at her, I knew by the way her eyes twinkled that she was smiling.

"I would take it off in the presence of my lover."

Underneath the soft clinging material of her wraparound her chest seemed to rise and fall faster. I could almost hear her heart beating. "Do you have a lover?" I asked.

She hesitated. "I've never been with a man, if that's what you want to know. For me it is forbidden."

"Why?"

She laughed. "Still asking questions. Be patient and all of your questions may be answered."

A soft chiming from the flight-computer made her look at the instrument panel. "We are entering city-limits. Our craft will land in a few moments, and we will have to register our arrival. Let me do the talking."

We landed next to a flat, squat building. There were no runways. All the aircraft were equipped with anti-grav lifters, which allowed for vertical takeoff and landing. I have been to some planets where they did actually need runways for their planes to land, because they did not have anti-grav technology. Anti-gravity generators were expensive to build and were just not affordable on some planets.

A pair of grim looking black-clad officials approached us. Skyla handed them a plastic card, which they scanned with a handheld device. "Bay G58 has been reserved for you. Leave your craft unlocked," one of them told her. He looked at me. "ID chip!" he barked.

I pointed to my ear. He made a move with his scanner.

"He is in my employ," Skyla told him.

He bowed slightly. "My apology. Proceed."

We taxied toward the squat building, entered it through a large gate. A tunnel led us underground into a parking area. G58 was three levels down. Most bays were occupied by craft similar to ours. After parking our vehicle, we took an elevator to *Level One*, where we boarded an underground passenger train.

"No private flying craft allowed within city-limits. Only government and emergency vehicles," Skyla explained.

It was crowded inside the train, but we managed to find a couple of empty seats. I've never liked underground transportation systems. To be below ground and in the company of so many people made me feel claustrophobic. A spacer, who is used to spending weeks, maybe months, cooped up inside a hollow can, surrounded by nothing but vacuum, having an attack of claustrophobia may seem strange, but somehow the emptiness of space was more soothing than the threat of being crushed by a collapsing tunnel.

When I looked around at the other passengers, I didn't see anyone else with similar reactions. So I closed my eyes, let the gentle vibrations of the moving train lull me into a restful state.

* * * *

Suddenly, *He* was there. His golden skin shone brightly in the fire of an alien sun. His wings half-spread he stood looking at me with a sad smile. "You cannot enter," he said. "Not yet."

"Why not?" I asked.

"Your time of banishment has not come to an end."

"But I grow tired," I said. "I feel lonely."

He laughed. "You've spread your seed through half the galaxy. How can you be lonely?"

"But I am. I need the companionship of my own kind. I need to be worshipped."

"You mean you need power. You need to rule. That desire has been your downfall."

"I need to be loved," I said.

"Loved?" His laughter was mocking. "Love is not what you seek; it is carnal pleasures."

"Isn't that what every mortal pursues?" I asked.

"You are not mortal."

"No, I am not. Immortality has been my curse. Time is moving slow in this timeline."

My perspective shifted. I saw a majestic figure with golden skin. Velvety, black wings sprouted from wide shoulders. Piercing eyes burned with living fire.

"Time has not changed you," I said with the voice of the Golden God. "You are still arrogant and ambitious."

"That may be so. But I also possess passion and the ability to love."

My perspective shifted again. I looked upon two golden-skinned beings. They were beautiful beyond description. One had wings covered with feathers of shiny gold, while the wings of the other one were as black as the darkness of space.

Two immortals.

Two brothers.

Light and dark.

Order and Chaos.

"You challenged the gods," the golden winged one said.

"I am a god," said the other one.

* * * *

A hand touched my shoulder. I was awake in an instant. Instinctively my hand reached for the knife in my boot.

The gentle motion of the train had stopped. "Time to get off," Skyla's voice said softly beside my ear.

Chapter Twenty-two

Somehow, I had suspected it. Skyla's father was not human; he was Ra-el-marras. When I looked into his golden eyes, I knew. No wonder she had been so curious about inter-racial marriages on other planets.

"You must be the Outsider John told me about," he said when Skyla introduced me.

"I guess I'm a marked man," I said.

He smiled. "It is not every day we get someone from the Outside visiting."

"I'm not exactly a visitor." I smiled back at him. "Sometimes I feel like a prisoner."

His eyes narrowed slightly. "You *did* drop in uninvited. Our defense grid could have destroyed your ship."

"It could have." I felt agreeable. "Except I don't know why it should have. My ship is only a merchant vessel, not a warship. You people are very secretive. One wonders why."

His golden eyes studied me. "You have a familiar look about you. It seems I've seen you before, somewhere."

I shrugged, grinned. "If you were from my corner of the Galaxy I'd say you've seen my face on the news grid. I've had some bad publicity."

"But I'm not from, as you put it, your corner of the Galaxy." His eyes twinkled suddenly. "Forgive me for being so rude. You are my daughter's guest. Sometimes my position and the work that I do spills over into my private life."

"What do you do?" I asked, trying to be polite.

"I'm an administrator with the State church."

"The Believers?"

He smiled. "That's what the people call it. It really doesn't have a name. We believe in *His* return."

"The Golden God." I nodded. "I understand that not all people on Ramarra belong to your church. There are the Gate-Keepers?"

"Their religion is older than ours. Essentially, we all believe in the same thing. There is only one difference: we welcome the returning god, while they want to keep him from entering the Gates."

I was going to ask him the same question I had already put to Skyla, but decided against it. She had evaded the answer; he probably would, too. Skyla had disappeared after introducing me to her father. She came back into the room, with another woman in tow.

"My mother," Skyla said.

"I am Sky." The woman spoke with a soft voice. She was veiled, like her daughter, but her veil was transparent, and I could see her face quite clearly. She smiled. "Older women are allowed to show their face to strangers," she said, as if reading my mind.

I touched my lips, made a small bow. "The light in your eyes rivals that of the sun," I said, hoping I remembered it correctly.

"No need to be formal." She laughed. "But it is nice to hear it again. It's been a long time since somebody said that to me."

"I hope I didn't say anything offensive," I said, looking at her husband.

He laughed, waved with one hand. "She's always been a romantic, my wife. It's her human heritage. We don't use that phrase anymore."

"I have prepared some food," Sky said. She looked at her daughter. "I hope you'll stay long enough to join us for dinner."

Skyla nodded. "I don't have to report until later this afternoon. There is enough time."

The dining room had a large window, and when I looked out, I saw a mountain ridge in the distance. "You have a beautiful view," I commented.

"My husband's position allows us to have better living quarters than most people enjoy. We are on the 57th floor, and there are no other high buildings between the mountains and us. We are lucky." Sky touched her husband's hand. "I am lucky. Raktar has given up much of his private life to make this possible. But sometimes I wish he wouldn't work so hard."

Raktar smiled at her. "I don't mind. Some day we will have even a better life than this. When *He* returns *He* will know that I've been a faithful servant."

"You certainly have." She looked at me. "Are you a religious man, Thomas?"

I shrugged. "I believe in myself. I believe in life. I believe in enjoying life. But I don't worship any gods."

"We'd like you to come with us to one of our worship services." She had removed her veil for dinner; her eyes were bright and shiny. "Some of our *Promised Virgins* will be initiated tonight. Taking part in this celebration may plant a small seed of faith inside you. You will find that we also worship life."

I didn't really feel like going to a place of worship. Watching a bunch of religious fanatics perform their theatrics might be somewhat amusing, but also boring. I could think of better things to spend an evening.

"Go with them," Skyla said. "My father is a very influential man. Going to the temple will not be to your disadvantage."

"Alright," I said. "I accept your invitation. I am honored."

Sky put her hand on my arm. "You honor us by accepting. Skyla is right; Raktar has great influence with certain people." Her hand lingered a little bit too long on my arm, making me feel uncomfortable. It wouldn't be a good idea to fool around with the wife of a man who had connections to the church and the State.

"Do you have plans for me this afternoon?" I asked Skyla.

She shook her head. "No. I was hoping you'd keep my parents company."

"I have to go back to work," Raktar said. "A minor problem that needs to be dealt with." He looked at his wife. "I guess it is your job then to keep our guest entertained." He rose and smiled at me. "Don't tell my wife too many secrets about the Outside. She is a very curious woman, just like her daughter."

"I'll come with you, father," Skyla said. "You can drop me off." Turning to me, she said, "He has his own government flyer. I hate those crowded trains."

After they left I helped Sky with cleaning up the dishes. The plates and cups went into a recycler, so did the leftover food. Only the cutlery needed to be washed. It didn't take long until we went back into the living room.

"Sit over there," Sky told me, pointing to a wide chair. When I followed her invitation she knelled in front of me, her eyes bright and her face flushed. "My husband doesn't really have important business to deal with," she said.

"I don't understand."

Her hands felt hot on my thighs. I could feel myself reacting to her intimate touch.

"You are not really familiar with our customs, are you, Thomas?"

"Not really."

She opened her gown. Her breasts were white and round; her nipples short, but thick. She rose, straddled me and pressed her breasts into my face. "Taste them," she said, her breath coming fast.

I took one of her nipples into my mouth, sucked on it.

"That feels good," she moaned her hands busy in my lap.

I licked the salty perspiration from the cleavage between her breasts, inhaled the fragrance of her femininity. She was a mature woman, but her breasts were solid, her body firm. My freed member throbbed hard in her hand. She lifted up, pushed back down. I slid into creamy softness. She let out a deep sigh and began to rotate her pelvis.

"Does your husband know about this?" I asked, suppressing a loud moan.

Snapping her hips back and forth, she whimpered, clamped down hard. I felt warm liquid running onto my thighs. "He may suspect," she said between clenched teeth and rose, freeing my hard member. With flying fingers she practically ripped off my shirt, then my boots and pants. Flinging away her robe, she lay naked on the carpeted floor, her legs wide open. Between them her vagina was a pink flower, bare, except for a thin strip of hair above it.

"Come, hurry," she said, her fingers fluttering an invitation.

Dropping between her white thighs, I guided my penis toward her pink orifice, touched the engorged tip to her thick labia. She moaned and curled her fingers around my hardness; lifting her hips off the floor, she pulled. Again, I slid easily into her, pushing deep.

We didn't speak for a long time, letting our bodies do the talking. She was passionate, starved for sex, or so it seemed. Slamming her body against mine, she displayed a ferocity I had not expected in her gentle demeanor.

I came inside her with a loud roar, not caring if anyone heard. This was a welcome release of the tension that had been building up inside me these last few days. My encounter with the Makkala had been different. Whatever she was, the Makkala was not human; there had not been the raw emotion Sky was showing, and she had not come the way Sky was coming.

We had fucked. That was all. No emotion. No body fluids. No passion.

"Let me be on top," Sky whispered.

I pulled out, lay on my back. She straddled me, hovered for a moment, and then she took me back inside. I finally got a chance to study and enjoy her body. She had a lovely face, straight features, no wrinkles. Dark smoldering eyes, full lips. Her breasts round and full, hardly sagging. The rest of her body shapely. The years had been kind to her.

She moved slowly now, having spent most of her passion. Her

dark eyes studied me. "You have the body of a god," she said. Her inner muscles fluttered gently, sending ripples of pleasure through my body.

"You don't look so bad yourself," I told her.

She smiled. "You know exactly what to say, don't you? I can't remember the last time my husband gave me a compliment."

"I guess he takes you for granted?"

"I'm just his wife. He spends more time with his mistress than with me."

"A mistress?"

She closed her eyes. Her pelvis moved slowly back and forth. I felt her vagina muscles tighten around my shaft, milking me gently. After a moment, she sighed and opened her eyes again. "It is the custom. Most married men have a mistress, sometimes two. There are more women than men, didn't you know?"

"I'm a stranger. I know very little about your world."

"You will learn." She lifted up, released my penis. Rising, she walked over to the couch and bent over. Looking back over her shoulder, she smiled an invitation.

I got up and positioned myself between her spread long legs. Stroking her plump buttocks, I parted them slightly. Her vagina lips were thick and puffed up below her puckering anus. She reached behind her, grabbed my rigid pole and pulled it forward. I watched as it extended her soft labia and slowly slid into her creamy tightness. She moaned and arched her back, and began pumping her lower torso and rotating her pelvis.

Putting my hands on her quivering hips, I pushed deep into her. When the pressure inside me became too much I held her tight, let go and roared my pleasure as I filled her womb again with my load. She whimpered, put her face in the pillows to muffle her loud cries, while experiencing her own orgasm.

After it was over, we stood quiet for a while, let our breathing become normal. Then I pulled out and went to sit in one of the big chairs. She straightened her body, stretched. Again I admired her curvy figure, her narrow waist and her long slim legs. The slight bulge in her belly didn't matter, it complimented her shapely, round buttocks.

She smiled. "You are studying me?"

"I've always enjoyed looking at beautiful women, and right now I'm enjoying myself very much."

Turning slowly, she presented her whole body to my view. "I like showing off my body," she said, "especially to someone who appreciates it." She looked at my lap. "You are still stiff."

I chuckled. "That is my curse, or maybe my blessing. Depends how you look at it. It takes a long time for me to be totally satisfied."

Laughing, she came closer, touched my penis. She bent and took it into her mouth, sucked on it. Releasing it, she looked up at me. "You are an unusual specimen of a man. I've never met anyone like you." She turned around, presenting her buttocks for a fleeting moment, and then she sank into my lap and impaled herself on my rigid member. Snapping her pelvis, she moved up and down.

I grabbed her breasts, squeezed them gently. "Slow," I whispered into her ear. "I like it slow. Don't tire yourself out."

She slowed down, sat quiet for a moment. Then she lifted up and turned, facing me. "I want to look at you when you come," she said. Climbing back into my lap, she put her legs over the padded chair rests and took me into her again. We moved very little after that, except for her vagina pulsing around my penis. Only when she came she went wild. Kissing me fiercely, she probed the cave of my mouth with her tongue.

Then she collapsed into my embrace. She clung to me for a long time, before she slipped from my lap.

"I'm taking a shower," she said. "Want to join me?"

I took her one more time in the shower. We were both satiated after that.

"I hope my husband doesn't ask for my services tonight," she said, chuckling. "I am a little sore."

Chapter Twenty-three

The temple was an impressive building, with domed roofs, high ceilings, massive pillars, and plenty of statues. Strange, how people always have the resources to built elaborate places of worship, even in bad times. Religious believers will sacrifice their last piece of bread to insure themselves a spot in a promised land. A place that may exist only in their imagination.

Skyla wasn't with us when we went to the temple, which was too bad, because it wouldn't have made me feel like a third wheel. Even though Sky's behavior was relaxed and immaculate, I couldn't help wondering if her husband suspected something. She was dressed in a long, flowing gown that complimented her slim figure. She looked absolutely delicious. A scarf made from some silky material covered her face and head.

Raktar looked splendid beside her in his ceremonial white robe. They did make a handsome couple.

I had borrowed one of Raktar's robes. It was a little tight around my shoulders, but I believe I didn't look too bad in it. Sky kept glancing at me, smiled when she felt unobserved. I was hoping Raktar wouldn't notice. The last thing I needed right now was an enemy in high places.

All the men wore robes. White was the predominant color, but some of the robes were red, black or purple.

The inside of the temple was huge, easily capable of holding a few thousand people. The pews were arranged in a circle around a raised platform, a stage. In the center of the stage, a large rectangular structure was clearly an altar.

We sat fairly close to the stage. Our seats were level with the top of the altar.

The place was filled to capacity. The majority of worshippers were women. Like in most places of worship, the crowd spoke only in hushed voices. It became quiet when a booming gong announced the beginning of the service.

I noticed movement on the side of the altar, which was facing us. A curtain parted, revealing a doorway. Out of the doorway stepped a figure dressed in a black robe. The priest, I assumed. The congregation rose, waited until the priest climbed up a set of steps that led to the top of the altar. He stood with his arms raised, began to chant in a language

I didn't understand.

Everybody sat down again. More figures came out of the door in the altar, spread out on the stage. I counted twenty-five. All wore white robes. All were female and young. None of them had her face or head covered.

They began swaying their bodies to music coming out of hidden speakers. Three of the girls shed their robes. Naked, they danced around the altar. One of the three caught my eye. She danced with exceptional grace; her body was slim and lithe, and her movements sensuous, almost sexual. And she had the most beautiful face.

The music stopped, the dancers froze. Out of the doorway stepped another figure--a man. From his broad shoulders hung a thick, golden cloak. It opened behind him like a pair of wings. He was big, well-muscled. Striding over to the group of girls he reached out, touched one. She took his hand, climbed with him to the top of the altar, where she slipped out of her robe and stood waiting, her naked breasts thrust forward.

She turned and looked at the priest. Chanting in a low voice, he put his hands on her breasts, her belly, and then between her legs. He stepped back and lifted his arms over his head.

A gong rang three times.

The girl turned again, faced the young man with the golden cloak. Sinking to the floor in front of him, she touched his huge erection, then she lay down and spread her legs wide. Her body began to rise, as if she were floating in the air. But I was close enough to see the thin metal rods coming out of the altar, supporting the small platform she lay on.

When her body was level with the cloaked man's rigid penis it stopped moving. The young man moved between her spread thighs. His buttocks snapped forward and under the loud booming of a bell he penetrated the girl's virginal vagina.

At least I assumed she was a virgin.

Beside me Sky seemed to be breathing a litter heavier than usual. She bent closer and whispered, "This ceremony is called *The Holy Creation of Life*. The young man represents the Golden God and the virgin all the women in the world. She is very lucky. She will bear the son of a god."

On the altar the priest stood beside the girl, holding her hands. Between her spread legs the *Golden God* moved with forceful thrusts. His wings had opened wide, fluttered as if in a breeze. They looked quite realistic in the strobe lighting from spotlights in the ceiling and floor.

He began to move faster, the music rose in volume, drums rolled, bells rang.

He stopped moving, only his buttocks quivered. The girl's buttocks lifted up, her belly worked feverishly.

The music had stopped. In the silence the girl's cries of ecstasy rang over speakers through the temple as she received the life-giving fluid. A gong sounded seven times, and then everything was thrown into darkness.

I almost cried out in surprise when a hand touched my crotch.

"Tomorrow I will take your gift again," Sky whispered into my ear. Her fingers curled around my penis and even the rough material of the robe didn't stop me from reacting. She chuckled and let go.

When the lights came back on, she sat properly beside me, her hands in her lap. Raktar, who sat on her other side, bent closer. "This is one of the most important celebrations," he said in a hushed voice. "I am glad you came with us to witness this."

I inclined my head. "I am honored to be here," I said. "It was most gracious of you to invite me."

"It was actually Skyla's idea. She wanted you to see it." Sky whispered.

On the stage a large number of white-robed females had assembled around the altar. The couple and the priest had disappeared. Music began to play softly. The girls started singing and chanting. They had beautiful, fine voices. As they sang, they let their robes fall to the floor and naked their bodies swayed with the music.

I found it quite odd that in a society where women walked around in public with their heads and faces covered, they would so freely display their nude bodies during a religious ceremony.

One of the girls separated herself from the rest. It was the same one I had admired before. She climbed the steps to the top of the altar, where she danced with graceful, sensuous movements. Her black hair hung down to her waist, flowed around her upper body like a transparent veil as she swirled to the chanting of the other girls.

Sky must have noticed me watching the girl. "She's beautiful, isn't she?" she whispered.

"Yes, she is," I agreed.

"She will be our next High Priestess; after she bears the Golden God's son."

I didn't comment. Whoever that young man was, the one who

represented the Golden God, he was a lucky man. All those beautiful young virgins he had to deflower and impregnate! And here I was-- spraying crops. Some people just have all the luck!

I noticed a number of figures in black robes taking positions on the stage. Members of the congregation began climbing up stairs that led onto the stage. They formed lines in front of the priests; there were four of them. Each held a rod in one hand. As the people walked past the priests, they would be touched on their forehead with the end of the rod.

"The *Sacred Blessing*," Sky murmured to me, as she and her husband got up to join one of the lines.

Obviously, since I wasn't a member, I couldn't be blessed. So I just sat there, watching. The girl on the altar was still dancing. She was truly beautiful, and I envied the priest who would sink his life-giver into her passionflower.

Actually, all the girls on the stage were lovely to look at. Slim bodies, pretty faces.

This was probably the only time men were allowed to see a young girl's face and nude body. Maybe that's why the congregation was so large.

Feeling bored, I got up and walking against the stream of worshippers. I found myself back in the entrance hall. There was more to this place than just the hall of worship, and I felt like exploring. Opening a door, I discovered a set of stairs leading to a lower level. On impulse, I climbed down the narrow steps and ended up in an empty room, with doors in each wall. One looked old, weathered. The hinges creaked when I opened it, and I entered a narrow corridor.

It smelled damp and musky. The lighting was bad and I stumbled over debris on the floor. It was obvious: this section of the temple was never used. At the end of the corridor was another door. It opened even more reluctantly than the first one.

Another set of stairs. One dim light in the wall illuminated the worn and slippery stone steps. I knew I probably shouldn't be here, but my sense of adventure would never allow me to turn back.

When I touched the wall it felt slimy, wet. My ears detected water dripping and my nose smelled the fungus growing on the walls.

I reached the bottom of the staircase. Ahead of me lay a cavern-like room. It was lit up by glowing panels in the ceiling. The walls were decorated with statues carved into the rock. Other statues stood on pillars, faded paintings covered the ceiling and part of the walls.

At the end of the cavern stood the oversized statue of the Golden God. To either side of him huge pillars framed a shimmering field of *Nothing* behind him.

I knew what it was.

A Gate.

The Golden God carried a large two-edged sword in one hand. His whole body glowed, and his eyes, by some trick of light, seemed alive.

There was a pulling inside my head when I looked at him. Deep inside me the darkness rumbled, stirred. I walked deeper into the room, stood looking up at the golden statue. This statue was old, older than the temple above. Older than anything I've seen so far.

He looked familiar. He was the Golden God from my dreams. His wings were half-open, as if ready to launch himself into the air.

I heard them before I saw them, recognized the sound of their clawed feet on the stone floor as they appeared from hidden niches in the walls. They surrounded me in silence, but didn't come close. I looked into their ugly flat faces, saw the gleaming canines as the creatures stared at me out of red eyes.

The rushing sound of displayed air from a pair of great wings made me turn my head.

She landed beside me, folded her shimmering butterfly-wings behind her. Her green eyes were large in her white, lovely face. "You cannot walk through the portal." Her voice was soft and sweet.

"Why not?" I challenged her.

"Because you are *shakka*. Banned."

"Why?"

She came closer. She looked like the winged girl I had encountered in the Old City, but she was not the same one.

"There is danger for you in this place," she said with a low voice. She ran a pink tongue across her sharp teeth. "My sister told me what she did. Are you seeking more pleasure?"

I touched her round breast. It felt soft and warm. "How did you and your minions get into this place?" I asked.

"Through there." She pointed to an oval, shimmering spot in the ceiling.

"A gate?" I said.

She nodded. "Yes. A portal."

"This one is a portal also," I said, indicating the square of *Nothingness* behind the golden statue. "Where does it lead?"

She smiled sadly. "To a place you can never enter."

"Who says so?"

"The Guardians. But you know that." She looked at me with those green eyes. "Why do you ask? Are you testing me?"

I studied her naked, lovely form. "Like your sister, you speak in riddles. You must have me confused with someone else. I've never been here before. Why would these so-called Guardians ban me from entering the gates? I don't know the Guardians and they don't know me. Or do they?"

"The portal is forbidden to you, my Lord." She almost whispered." She took my hand. "Come, I will give you pleasure. There is time, and it not forbidden."

She pulled me away from the portal, found a spot free of debris where she lay down with her legs open. Watching the couple on the altar had made me horny, and it wasn't hard for me to follow the Makkala's invitation. I took her forcefully under the watchful eyes of her ugly companions. She moved fiercely beneath me, but never uttered a sound of passion, not even when she experienced an orgasm. I know she did, because once in awhile a shudder would run through her body and her sex-organ would pulse strongly around my rigid penis.

"We must end it now," she said suddenly. "El-Makkala are coming."

I came inside her with a deep roar. I pulled out, helped her to her feet.

She touched my cheek, briefly, and whispered, "Thank you, my Lord." Then she rose into the air, disappeared through the shimmering oval in the ceiling. Her minions followed her on silent bat-wings.

Looking at the statue of the Golden God, I said, "I wonder who you are and who I am supposed to be, because I have no idea."

Chapter Twenty-four

Even though I was gone for a long time, my hosts had not been too concerned when they discovered me missing.

"I know these celebrations can drag on," Sky said after they found me waiting for them just outside the temple entrance.

"I didn't mean to be rude," I said, "but I've never been comfortable in large crowds and with religious ceremonies."

"Too bad you couldn't get the same ecstatic feeling we experienced."

I chuckled. "I had my share of ecstatic feelings, believe me."

"What did you do?"

"Not much. Just wandered around. These old buildings fascinate me. My mother is an archeologist. She studies vanished civilizations and their ruins. She got me interested."

"Did you know that this temple was built on top of an ancient holy site? There are passageways underneath the temple. Only the High Priests and chosen members of the Guardian Council are allowed to enter there. But even they shun most of the chambers. It is rumored that ferocious creatures that are neither dead nor alive inhabit them. And then there are the Makkala, an ancient race of supernatural beings. They will drink your soul, leave your body an empty shell."

"You talk too much." Raktar spoke sharply. "You humans are so superstitious." He turned to me. "Not only is she human; she is also a female. Believes everything." Sky didn't comment, but I could see her eyes flashing behind the thin veil.

"Sometimes there is a lot of truth behind rumors," I said.

"And much is total nonsense," Raktar snorted. "There is nothing underneath the temple that could be of possible interest to anyone."

Sky gave a little laugh. "No need to get yourself all worked up about this, my dear. If there is nothing in those underground caverns then I didn't give away any secrets."

"That is not the point. You have to be more careful what you say. Remember, the Guardian Council has watchers everywhere." Raktar spoke in a low voice. "I have my position to consider."

"I know. I know. Your precious position." She hooked her arm into mine. "Come, Thomas, you can take me home. My husband has some more important church-business to take care of. You can pilot the flyer, can't you?"

"I believe I'll manage." I smiled.

"Then it's settled." We began walking toward the parking garage. She stopped halfway across the street. "You know, I am not really tired. Why don't we go for a little stroll? It is warm and the moon is full."

There was a full moon, but we could barely see it, because of the bright streetlights. "Let's go to the park," Sky said, "we'll be able to look at the stars."

We walked past shops and stores. They were all closed. "Nobody goes shopping at night?" I asked.

Sky shook her head and laughed. "How can they? None of the stores are open."

"Never?"

"Never. Nights are for sleeping. Evenings are for relaxing, visiting and worshipping."

"On some planets stores never close."

She looked at me sideways. "That must be terrible. When do the people get time to socialize?"

I shrugged. "I really don't know. I've never been much for socializing myself. Spent most of my time in space."

"As a merchant you must meet a lot of different people?"

"I do, but I don't make friends very easily. One might say I am a loner."

"Hard to believe. A good looking, handsome man like you? I bet women just flock to you."

It was my turn to chuckle. "That still doesn't make me a sociable person."

"You've known many women?"

"How many is many?" I shrugged. "There have been a few in my life. None could keep me. I can't be domesticated."

Sky laughed and stroked my arm. "The right woman can *domesticate* any man."

We left the busy street, turned into a side street. The paved road ended after awhile, became a gravel path. There was an open gate. It was lit up by a couple of lights. After that we walked in darkness under tall trees. Through the branches I could see the stars and one of the moons. As my eyes adjusted to the light-conditions, I found it bright enough to see where we were going.

Sky took a deep breath beside me. "I love the outdoors," she said, almost dreamily. "I grew up in the country. I don't really care much for the life in the city. But these days I rarely get away anymore." She

139

stopped, stepped in front of me. Her arms went around my neck; she pulled me closer, lifted her veil and kissed me. After breaking the kiss, she whispered, "I'm glad you're here. This is a welcome break in my boring life."

"I gather you're not happy. Problems in your marriage?"

"My marriage is fine. But between his work and his mistress Raktar doesn't have much time left for me.'

"Your husband is Ra-el-marras. I get the impression he doesn't have much respect for humans."

"The Ra-el-marras were here first. According to their legends, the ancient Guardians brought them here. We humans are the intruders."

"Where do the Ra-el-marras come from? If this isn't their home-planet they must exist somewhere else."

Sky shrugged. "They don't know themselves. The origin of their race is lost in the past. I've studied their religious history books. There was an interesting chapter that mentions a race of immortals, who ruled the Galaxy since the dawn of time. One day they all disappeared. Apparently, they got bored with living in the physical world and entered a state of spiritual existence. The Ra-el-marras were their faithful servants and were chosen to guard the portals which lead to their spiritual world."

"And these portals are here on Ramarra?"

Sky was silent for a moment. While we talked we had been walking down the graveled path. We had arrived at a small pond. In the middle of it, standing on a pedestal, was the statue of a winged man-- the Golden God. He looked impressive, but not as life-like as the one I had seen down in the cavern.

There was a bench. Sky sat down, padded the seat beside her. She had taken off her veil. Her eyes reflected the bright light of the moon. "I don't think anyone can overhear us here," she said softly, looking up at me. "I've never seen these portals, but the history books described a location, which I believe is somewhere under the temple in this city. I've talked to Raktar about it, but he denies it. He tells me to stop prying into things that don't concern me."

I sat down beside her. "When we were transported from your colony on the moon to Ramarra, we used a gate. Is this technology part of the secrets your government is trying to protect? Is that why you have no contact with the rest of the Galaxy?"

She shook her head. "I don't know. It is possible. We don't question the decisions of the Guardian Council. None dare to speak out for fear of being punished."

"The Golden God. Who is he?"

"He is said to be a High Prince of the ancient race of immortals."

"How about the other one?"

"Which other one?"

"The Golden God with the black wings."

"How do you know about him? I thought you knew nothing about our religion?"

"I've seen him in my dreams."

She became silent again. Her eyes were on the statue in the pond. "You are an enigma, Thomas. Your sexual prowess; your mysterious arrival here. You travel in the company of two equally mysterious non-human women. And you ask a lot of questions." She chuckled when she saw my surprised look. "I requested your file from my father. Did you really think I'd let a complete stranger into my home before checking him out?"

I smiled. "And you say I am an enigma."

"I am just curious. I need to know things--and I live here. But I wonder why you are here. So does my father. You asked about the black-winged one. He is the *Prince of Darkness*, the Immortal who rebelled, the one who wanted to rule the heavens. The one the Guardians banned from entering the portal, because he chose chaos instead of order, war instead of peace, the pleasures of the flesh instead of spiritual enlightenment."

She paused. Her eyes were still studying the statue in the pond. "There is a secret cult among us. Its members worship him. He is the one the Ra-el-marras are guarding the portals against--the god who is cursed to wander the realm of the physical world until the end of time."

"You know a lot about him."

She looked at me. Her face lay in shadow. "I do, don't I."

"I am a little confused. Skyla told me that the Believers and the Gatekeepers believe in the same deity--the Golden God. You are telling me there are really two gods?"

She lowered her voice when she answered. "What I am telling you is not common knowledge. If anyone hears us, I could be severely punished by the Enforcers of the Guardian Council, for spreading heresy. Before the humans came, there was only one religion on Ramarra. The religion of the Gatekeepers. They never worshipped the *Prince of Darkness*, nor did they worship the prince with the golden wings, because they were never considered gods. The Gatekeepers existed only to guard the portals. Humans brought with them many beliefs. When they saw the numerous statues of the golden winged man, they made him into a god. Over time the teachings of the Ra-el-marras were woven into the beliefs of the humans. New doctrines were written. The Ra-el-marras and the humans adopted these new beliefs. The prince with the black wings was ignored, forgotten, rejected. But not by all. Some began to worship him. A secret religion was created. When *He* returns *He* will be welcomed, not rejected."

"So the god the Believers worship exists only in their imagination." I didn't make it a question.

"Don't all gods?" she asked.

"I'm surprised to hear you say that. I thought you were a strong believer."

"I am, but I worship a different god."

"Who might that be?"

She looked at me from the side. "I think you know. Just like him I worship the pleasures of the flesh."

"So do I. But that is all I worship. I don't worship any gods." I put an arm around her shoulders, pulled her close.

She leaned her head against mine. "Let's go home," she said. "We'll worship together. My husband won't be home till tomorrow night." Before we could rise, I heard the sound of boots on gravel. Three bulky figures wearing black cloaks stepped in front of us. I saw the glint of some kind of weapon in the hands of one of them.

"Guardian Enforcers!" Sky whispered.

"You will come with us!" The one with the weapon spoke harshly.

"Where are you taking us?" I asked.

"You don't ask the questions here!" he barked.

"Then tell me why you are arresting us."

He lifted his weapon and pointed it at me. It was obviously some kind of gun. "Be silent. You know why. You and this woman are guilty of blasphemy."

"You are mistaken. We were just raising hypothetical questions. Whatever you may have heard, you are misinterpreting it." Sky raised her voice. "Do you know who I am?"

"We know who you are. You are the wife of Raktar, one of the church administrators."

"Then you know that I am a devoted Believer. My husband will verify that."

He laughed. "It was your husband who told us to follow you. He's suspected you for a long time."

"My husband loves me. He would never betray me like this."

"Your husband is a devoted administrator of the State-Church. He puts the laws of the Church above anything else, even his feelings for you." He waved his gun. "Now, get up and kneel over there!"

"What will they do to us?" I asked Sky in a low voice.

"The punishment for spreading heresy is imprisonment."

The gunman laughed. "Not this time. We have other orders."

"Kill them already, before someone comes," said one of the other two. The Darkness inside me took over my body and mind. I moved without conscious thought. The knife was in my hand. Blood spurted from a severed artery as the sharp blade flashed sideways. Vaulting over the collapsing body of the Enforcer I moved the knife in a circular motion, cutting the heart out of the second man's chest. The third one died as the molecular disrupter in the blade shattered his skull. It was over in seconds.

Sky stared in shock at the three lifeless bodies, then at me. "You killed them!" she gasped hysterically.

The knife was still glowing in my hand. I bent to put it back in its sheath in my boot. "You heard it yourself—they would have killed us." My voice sounded hollow and gravelly.

"Your eyes!" Sky exclaimed, shrinking back, suddenly afraid of me. "What are you?" she asked.

Deep inside me the Darkness was still there. Lately it was never truly gone. "I don't know," I told her and gave her a reassuring smile. "But you don't have to fear me."

"I've never seen anyone move so fast," she said, getting back her composure. "Are you genetically enhanced?"

I shrugged. "I'm not aware of it. I've no memory of my youth."

"You don't remember your childhood?"

"No. As far as I can remember, I always looked like this. Maybe I was never young."

"Are you an artificial?"

"I don't believe so." I held out a hand. "Come. We must get away from here as quickly as possible."

Chapter Twenty-five

Raktar came home early in the morning. Sky and I were just having breakfast. Lucky for us, we were dressed.

"How nice to have you home so soon. I didn't expect you until late tonight." Sky acted cheerful, gave him a quick kiss on the cheek. "I guess things went well for you?"

At first, he glared at her, and then his expression changed. "Not as well as I had hoped. I'll just have to deal with it. And you? Everything alright?"

"I'm fine, dear."

He looked at me. "How about you, Thomas Stone? Did you have a satisfactory time last evening?"

I treated him with a big smile. "As a matter of fact, I did. In my travels, I've experienced different, exciting things. There is something new on every planet, and some things never change. Yours is no exception."

"They found three dead Guardian Enforcers last night, in the park near the temple. But I guess you wouldn't have heard about it--yet."

"That is terrible." Sky went to get a cup for her husband. "Any ideas what happened?"

"We have our suspicions. Nothing concrete. But we'll find the murderers."

"Who would dare to defy one of the Guardian Enforcers? Never mind killing one." Sky gave her husband a sidelong glance.

He took a sip from his cup, his eyes resting on me. "Who indeed?"

"Are you involved in the investigation of the murders?" I asked.

"Yes, I am."

"I thought you were an administrator for the Church, not a criminal investigator."

"One of the dead men was good friend of mine. I asked to be involved."

"How would you know about it so soon?" asked Sky.

"I was the one who found them. There were some things that had been bothering me, so I went for a walk in the park. To clear my mind." He emptied his cup and got up. "Skyla will be coming home soon. I assume you are going back with her, Stone?"

I was aware of the impersonal tone he was using. Nodding, I said, "My employer is probably anxious to have me back. I was surprised he gave me time off to come here."

Sky chuckled. "He is our daughter's grandfather. How could he refuse her wishes?"

"She is too stubborn for own good, sometimes. Must be the human genes in her." Raktar said.

"It always is, isn't it?" Sky walked back into the kitchen, leaving us alone.

"Why did you marry a human if you hate them so much?" I asked him.

Raktar snorted. His golden eyes were dark when he looked at me. "You are a visitor to our planet. A stranger. What would you know about us. Before the humans came, the Ra-el-marras had a single purpose. We were one people. Now we are divided. The humans brought with them different ideas, different beliefs. We have two major religions and who knows how many forbidden minor ones. Now--here you are, bringing new ideas and concepts. I don't believe you're just a simple merchant."

I smiled. "Why would you think that?"

"The way you talk, the way you behave. There is something arrogant and menacing about you. I believe your presence here will have unpleasant consequences. I see the way my wife looks at you."

"It's my animal magnetism." I grinned. "I'm used to having women admire me. But you are wrong about one thing. I am no menace to you, or to anyone who doesn't threaten me."

"And the ones who threaten you?"

"They wish they never had." I smiled. "But what are you afraid of? You're not threatening me, are you?"

Sky came back into the dining room, smiled. "Are you staying home tonight, dear?" she asked her husband.

Again he gave her this glaring look. "What if I am?"

"Just asking. By the way, I'll be going with Skyla to visit my father. It's been awhile since I saw him. I hope you don't mind?"

"Why should I? You're not a prisoner here."

"We are all prisoners of something," she said sullenly.

"Watch what you say," her husband warned her. "You never know where the Guardian Enforcers have their spy-eyes."

"Surely not in our own home?" Sky looked aghast.

"They can be anywhere. Even inside your own house. The Guardian Council is aware of everything. When will you ever realize that?"

A soft chiming sound interrupted us.

"Ah, that must be our daughter," Sky said, heaving a deep sigh.

She was right. Moments later the door opened and Skyla walked in. She gave her father a quick hug and her mother a kiss on the cheek. Then she nodded toward me. "I hope you and my father didn't butt heads too much. He is very Ra-el-marras, and not too fond of humans." She looked at Sky. "Except for my mother, of course."

Sky laughed. "Child. You misjudge your father. He doesn't hate humans. If he did, he would have never risen to the position of High-Administrator." She looked at Raktar. "Isn't that so, dear? We have to be careful what we say. Rumors like that could be disastrous."

"Nobody would believe it. After all--I am the High-Administrator of the State-Church." Raktar smiled at his daughter. "Your mother is going with you to visit your grandfather. Don't let her get into any trouble."

"I'll keep an eye on her, Father." The girl laughed, gave him another hug. "I love you. You behave yourself when we are away. And don't work too hard. We'll be back in a couple of quarter-cycles."

"Make sure you're back. An important day is coming up." He stroked her hair and kissed her on the forehead.

"Don't worry, Father. I'll be here."

Sky seemed to be in a hurry to get away. She had her things packed in a short time. We left as soon as she was ready. I was surprised we made it out of the city unmolested. I guess Raktar's influence wasn't as great as I had assumed, but I didn't relax too much and stayed alert, watching the sky above and the ground below us.

"Does this thing have any built-in weapons?" I asked.

Skyla laughed. "No. Whatever for?"

"Don't travelers ever get robbed?"

"I've never heard of such a thing. We carry nothing anybody would want."

"Are you telling me that you don't have any criminals on this planet?"

"There are criminals. Most of them have committed crimes against the government or church, hardly against individual people." Sky answered for her daughter. "Of course, I can't speak for Arenia. Things might be different there."

"Why are you suddenly so anxious to visit Grandfather?" Sky asked her mother. "You hardly communicate with him anymore."

Sky looked at her daughter, took her hand into hers. "There is something I must tell you, Skyla. A terrible thing has happened. Your father wants me dead."

Skyla pulled her hand away. "I don't believe you, Mother."

"I didn't think you would. Nevertheless, it is true. Ask Thomas."

I put the craft on autopilot and swiveled around in my chair. Skyla was staring at me. "We have no direct proof," I said, "but it is highly likely. There was an attempt on your mother's life last night."

"If it hadn't been for Thomas, I'd be dead now," Sky said.

Skyla put her hands over her eyes. "Father would never do that. He loves you."

"Our marriage is not what it seems. Your father hates humans, including me."

"I don't believe that!" Sky said fiercely, her gold-flecked eyes burning. "I know he doesn't exactly love humans, but he would not commit murder. You must be wrong!"

"I wish it were so." Sky sighed. "You see, I don't hate your father. There was a time when I loved him. And I thought he loved me, too. Now--I'm not so sure anymore."

"You're wrong. You have to be. Thomas said you have no proof."

"No concrete proof. What I am going to tell you will incriminate me and Thomas." She looked at me.

I nodded. "Go ahead."

"Last night, after the celebration, Thomas and I went for a walk in the park beside the temple. There three Guardian Enforcers approached us. They had orders to kill us. The orders came from your father."

Skyla shook her head, but said nothing.

"They told us that. I would not lie to you, my daughter."

"Why would Father want to have you murdered?" Skyla's voice was but a whisper.

Sky shrugged. "Maybe because he found out about me. I broke the law, and so have you."

Sky gasped behind her veil. "I haven't done anything, Mother."

"No, you haven't. But you are guilty by association."

"How would he even know?"

"He has spies. Don't forget, he is a man who has great influence."

"How did you...I mean...you are here. What happened?"

"Thomas killed the assassins."

Skyla gave a little shriek. "But they were Guardian Enforcers! You are marked now. They will hunt you down."

"It happened in the park, at night. There were no witnesses."

"How about the surveillance cameras?"

"That part of the park is free of them. You know where it is: the pond with the statue of the Golden God. Your father told me about the absence of surveillance cameras and audio pick-ups. Many high-ranking government officials go there to reflect. They want to be unobserved. I visit there frequently. Your father knows that."

Skyla looked at me. "How was it possible for you to defeat three Enforcers? They are trained professionals."

I gave her a grim smile. "So am I."

"You should have seen him," Sky said. "He moved with the speed of a cavern-serpent. There is more to our Thomas here than he is telling us." She put her hand on mine. "Whatever it is, I am glad you were there with me."

Skyla looked at both of us for moment, a crease on her forehead, and then she leaned back into her seat. She didn't say anything for the rest of the trip, which was fine by me. I had my own problems to mull over.

What if Sky was wrong and there had been surveillance cameras? After all--it was her husband who had told her there weren't any. The computer would identify us quickly. If that happened, I was in deep trouble, with no way to get off this planet. I didn't even know if they had any shuttles that were capable of traveling in space. We had arrived here via a portal--a teleportation device.

The knowledge of these portals was already enough reason to keep me from ever leaving this planet.

Ramarra. Portal.

This was an ancient world with a hidden secret. A secret I had to uncover.

The Golden God.

The Ra-el-marras.

The Makkala.

The Gates.

Deep inside me, the Darkness stirred. Not for the first time I wondered.

I had my own secret to unmask. They had done tests. Many tests. To expose my hidden past. To find out who I was, what I was. They confirmed I was human, at least my body was, or seemed to be. But what about my mind, that energy which kept this body functioning and put it above the level of animals? What about that?

They had tested it, too. My brainwaves, my thought-patterns, my

IQ. All had been normal. A little above average, but normal.

I never told anyone about the Darkness. It was beyond my control, surfacing in times of stress and danger. It was not an alien mind, not a symbiont, of that I was certain. When it took over my body, it did not push aside my identity. To the contrary--it made my mind sharper, clearer, made me more alive, almost jubilant.

"Thomas, are you sleeping?"

A hand shook my shoulder. It was Skyla. She had climbed into the copilot's seat. "You want me to take over the controls for awhile?" she asked.

I shook my head. "No, I'm fine. Just daydreaming. How about you?"

"I'm fine, too. Thank you."

Chapter Twenty-six

My old Sprayer had been repaired. I was a little apprehensive when I took it out the first time, wondering if any of the damaged parts had been replaced, or just patched up. I need not have worried, everything worked fine.

Crollin, my co-pilot, seemed uneasy in my presence. He kept throwing sidelong glances at me. "Concentrate on your work," I told him, when he forgot to turn off the spray-jets as we flew over a small lake.

"Sorry," he apologized.

"Is something bothering you?" I asked.

He shook his head; his eyes were large behind the protective goggles.

"I'm not going to change into some kind of monstrous creature and take your soul," I said.

"You were with the Makkala." His tone was accusing. "You say you are human, but no human is allowed to enter the ancient Holy Places, only Ra-el-marras can. Are you a High Priest?"

I laughed. "I can ease your fears right there. I'm neither Ra-el-marras, nor am I a priest."

He worked his controls without looking at me. Even though the air conditioning unit was working perfectly, beads of perspiration glistened on his exposed forehead. Shrugging, I turned my attention back to my instrument panel. I couldn't tell him any more than I told anyone else who asked me that same question.

We didn't talk much for the rest of the day, but then again, Crollin had never been much of a talker. As long as he performed his duty to my satisfaction, I had no problem with that.

* * * *

Three days after I had come back from the city, I got a visit from Sky. She came to my room in the evening. I asked her to sit on the only chair. She sat down, removed her veil and smiled. "I can't stay," she answered my unspoken question.

"A guy can hope." I grinned. "How are you holding up?"

"Fine, thank you. And you?"

"I'm alright. But I must admit, I am wondering what is going to happen to you when you go back."

She shrugged. "Maybe I won't go back. We'll see."

I looked at her. She was so beautiful, and I felt like taking her into my arms. "Why did you come?" I asked.

"I wanted to ask you if you'd be interested in coming with me to one of our worship services." She smiled, hesitated. "Remember, I told you about a secret cult? I am a member of that cult. We worship the Golden God with the black wings."

"This cult is forbidden?" I asked.

She nodded. "Yes, but we are numerous. Soon we may not be meeting in secrecy anymore."

"Your fellow members can't give you protection?"

"Maybe my god can." Her eyes were bright when she looked at me. "Please, come."

"Alright. When?"

"Tomorrow. I asked my father to give you the day off."

I lifted an eyebrow. "You're certainly sure of your persuasive abilities. I may not have agreed to come. Or maybe you know me too well."

She smiled. "I do."

"I'm surprised your father lets me go. At this rate I'll never work off my debt."

She gave me a long look. "I don't believe you ever will, no matter how much you work."

"Someone else already told me that," I said.

She rose. "I'll send for you in the morning."

"What should I wear?" I asked.

"It doesn't matter. We are not that rigid in our ceremonies." Before she covered her face, she gave me a big smile. "You'll see." Then she turned and walked out of the door. I watched her go, a beautiful woman who deserved better than she got.

* * * *

It was Skyla who came to get me. She was dressed in a loose, flowing robe. Even though only a thin veil covered her head and face, I still couldn't see what she looked like underneath.

We used the same Flyer we had used before. It was a beautiful day, the sun shone brightly, bathing the fields below with a golden light. It seemed a shame to spend the day inside a stuffy building with a bunch of cult members, worshipping a god they had created themselves. Sky had told me herself that before the humans came the black-winged man had not been considered a god.

After a two-hour flight, we ended up in one of the smaller cities.

Control didn't seem to be as tight as in the big city. Nobody challenged us or told us to leave our craft at the edge of the city. We landed near a large, plain looking building. There was no sign that this was some kind of temple or church. Of the other Flyers already parked there, none was government-owned.

When we entered the building, we found ourselves inside a warehouse. Sky led us down a dark corridor. A door at the other end opened into a narrow staircase. At the bottom another corridor, and then we stepped into a small room.

Skyla opened one of the doors in the opposite wall. There was nothing behind it but a glimmering field.

A Gate.

We stepped through it. The cavern we appeared in was not as huge as the one under the temple, but still quite large.

The golden statue of a black-winged man caught my attention.

"There he is," whispered Sky beside me. "Doesn't he look magnificent?"

He did. The statue was old, but not ancient, like the ones I had seen in the old city, and the one of the Golden God below the temple.

There were people kneeling in front of it. Sky pulled my hand. "Come, let's get closer."

"You go," I said. "I'm not kneeling in front of anyone, especially a statue." I smiled. "No offence."

"You don't have to kneel," she whispered.

I shook my head. "I'll watch from here. You two go."

"I'm staying with Thomas," Skyla said.

Sky looked at her daughter. "You'll have to make up your mind one way or the other," she told her. "And soon."

"I know, Mother," Skyla said. "But not today."

I watched Sky walk toward the statue. She was a graceful woman, tall and slim. And beautiful. I cursed her husband for wanting to end her life.

When she arrived at the food of the statue, she knelt for a short moment, and then she rose and walked over to a group of worshippers on the other side.

I looked around the cavern. Bright panels in the ceiling illuminated the interior with a diffused light. Thick curtains covered parts of the walls, and faded paintings adorned the naked rock that wasn't covered. One of the curtains parted, and two figures dressed in black robes walked slowly toward the group of worshippers. Each carried a container shaped like an urn. When they reached the group of men and women, one produced a large chalice, which he filled with a dark liquid from one of the urns. The worshippers lined up to drink from the offered vessel.

"Do you want to learn more about my mother's religion?" Skyla asked beside me.

"Yes, I would."

She pulled me toward a curtain-covered wall. The curtain hid a door, which led us into another, smaller cavern. There were tables and chairs, and a few couches. One wall held a bookcase. I saw a great number of books on the shelves, most of them looked old and weathered.

"This is the library, where the scholars study the scriptures and the history of Old Earth." Skyla spoke in a hushed tone.

A couple of people sat at a table. They looked up when we entered, then turned back to their studies. I went to the bookcase, picked up one of the books. The leather covering was worn and cracked, but it opened easily. "The End of Religion," I read. It was written in *Amerenglish*, one of the old standard Earth languages. Only scholars, historians, and scientists studied it. My mother had taught me.

"Can you read this?" I asked Skyla.

She nodded. "Not very well, but I can." Handing me another book, she said, "Take a look at this one."

It held mostly pictures. Paintings and drawings.

On the first page was the painting of a golden-skinned man with black wings.

The next page began: He had been a Prince, a favorite among the Immortals. His empire spanned across hundreds of worlds, his armada of spaceships conquered planet after planet. There was no stopping him. He was an Immortal, and unchallenged he would become ruler over the whole Galaxy and beyond.

When his ambitions grew too high, the unseen Guardians, who serve neither good nor evil, decided to put an end to his reign.

They imprisoned his essence inside a golden statue, created in his image. His immortal body was cursed to wander the physical world forever, or until the Guardians decided to let him enter the world of the Immortals. Stripped of his powers, his mind connected by a fine threat to his life force, he wanders from star to star, lost in time and space.

One day he will return and claim his rightful place among the Immortals. When this day comes, we will welcome him as our Lord.

He is called the Prince of Darkness, the Deceiver, the Seducer, the Evil One.

He is neither.

He is the Lightbringer who delivers us from the shame, which demands that we cover our bodies and faces.

He delivers us from the belief that a man must not look at a woman with lust in his eyes.

He lets us shed our robes so men and women may join their bodies in the pursuance of the pleasures of the flesh...

* * * *

I looked at Skyla who had silently been watching me while I read. "This was never written on Earth," I said.

She shrugged. "I wouldn't know. Maybe only some of it was written on Earth. But that doesn't matter. What matters is the knowledge these books contain. Knowledge, which has been suppressed by the State Church."

"It's all about power, Skyla. Governments, the church included, tend to misuse it."

"Why?"

"Because they can." I smiled. "For the good of the people, they will tell you. Ignorant people are much easier to control than knowledgeable ones."

"It's all about control, then," she said.

"Pretty much."

A man in a black robe entered the room through another door. He gave me a nod when he saw me watching him, then he went over to the bookshelves and picked up a book. Before he could sit down at a table, Skyla had walked up to him. She spoke to him in a subdued voice, and then she pointed at me. He smiled and beckoned, indicating a chair on the other side of the table.

Following his invitation, I took the seat across from him.

"I am Brother Trovar. Skyla tells me you are a visitor to our world. From the Outside. Is that true?"

"It's true." I smiled. "My name is Thomas Stone."

"How did you get through our defense-grid?"

I shrugged. "My ship is just a small merchant vessel. No danger to anyone. Our jump-capacitors were damaged. Yours was the closest system to seek out for repairs."

"Maybe there was another reason for your appearance here." Brother Thomas smiled. "The Guardians have their own agenda."

154

"I thought you worshipped the black-winged god?"

"We do, but we also acknowledge the existence of the Guardians."

"Who are the Guardians?"

"Gods." He shrugged. "We don't know. The Ra-el-marras refer to them in their writings. They were worshipped by the ancient race of Immortals, who once ruled the Galaxy."

"They are still worshipped in parts of the Galaxy. Speaking of ancient civilizations, these Immortals, it seems they once populated this planet. I've been to one of their abandoned cities."

His eyes widened. "Not inside?"

I smiled. "I'm afraid I was."

He made a sign in the air in front of him. "What did you see?" he asked.

"A beautiful woman with the wings of a butterfly."

Staring at me, he whispered, "Makkala! No human survives an encounter with the Makkala. Who are you, Thomas Stone?"

"That question has been put to me many times lately. I can only tell you the same thing I tell everyone else. I am a simple man, just like you."

Shaking his head, he said, "Not so simple, it seems."

"Tell me about the portals," I said.

"You don't use them Outside?"

"No." I chuckled. "We still travel the slow way: Spaceships."

"I wasn't aware of that. I know very little about the Outside. Only what I read in the old books. What would you like to know?"

"This planet seems to be riddled with portals. But I can't imagine that the Ancients used them only to travel on Ramarra."

"Oh no, they didn't." He rose, went to the bookshelves. After a moment of searching, he pulled out a thick book. Sitting down again, he opened it and pushed it across the table toward me. "Here, look at these pictures."

The first picture showed a sparkling wheel, dotted with glowing stars. I recognized it for what it was: the Galaxy. Fine lines, like strands of a massive spider web crisscrossed the entire wheel.

"That's how they ruled the stars." Brother Trovar's voice was hushed, awed.

"That is why Ramarra is closed to outsiders. Whoever possesses the secret of the portals commands great powers." I looked at him.

He smiled, nodded. "Is that why you are here?" he asked.

The man was perceptive. "I didn't know about the portals, not until

I came here," I said, evading a direct answer. He'd know. I turned the pages. There were pictures of golden-winged people, pictures of golden cities with buildings spiraling into the sky. I saw the lovely forms of the Makkala gliding through the air on multicolored butterfly wings, hordes of their ugly minions surrounding them.

There were paintings of strange looking beings, clearly denizens of other planets. Some were human; some so bizarre one wondered how such beings came into existence.

"These are reproductions of paintings we found in caves, and also in the ancient ruins, which only the priests of the Ra-el-marras can enter," Brother Trovar explained.

"My mother would be ecstatic," I said. "She studies ancient civilizations."

Brother Trovar chuckled. "So you did have a mother. I assume she was human?"

"She was--is. However, she's not my real mother. I was adopted."

He sighed. "And here I thought I had your mystery solved." He rose. "You must excuse me. Duty calls." He hesitated. "Would you like to take part in our Celebration of Life?"

"I am not a member of your faith," I said.

"Don't worry about that. We are not that strict. All are welcome."

I looked at Skyla. She nodded and said, "Accept the invitation, Thomas. I wish I could." Her eyes were bright when she looked at me.

"Why don't you?" I asked her.

"I can't. Not yet." She gripped my hand. Her fingers trembled slightly. "Go, Thomas. Experience the enjoyment that awaits you."

Chapter Twenty-seven

I followed Brother Trovar into another room. On shelves along one wall, I saw bundles of clothing. Brother Trovar went to a closet and took out a red robe. He shook it out, handed it to me. "You're a big man, but this should fit you," he said, and added, "put your clothing over there." He pointed to the shelves.

He watched me strip, and when I was dressed in the robe he handed me a hood, told me to cover my head and then to follow him. We walked down a narrow corridor. Opening a door, he told me to join the others. When I stepped through the door, I found myself back in the large cavern, but close to the statue of the winged man. There were two groups of people standing in front of the statue; all of them wore robes, one group red, and the other one yellow. A priest in a black robe saw me coming, pointed at the group in red.

I did a quick count as I walked to join them. Twenty-two pairs of eyes watched me from behind narrow slits. Even though they had their faces covered, I was sure they all knew each other. A big man like me stands out in any crowd, and the robe didn't hide my size. They didn't say anything when I joined them, but one touched my sleeve in a gesture of welcome.

The Yellow Robes had been watching also. I didn't count them, but I could tell at first glance that they were in the majority.

"Let us begin the Celebration of Life." The priest's amplified voice sounded from speakers set into the base of the statue.

My companions took off their robes. As I already had suspected, all of them were males. Naked, they began walking toward the group in yellow robes. I followed them, not quite knowing what to do. Each of the men picked a partner. So did I. It was not a big surprise when the robe of the person I had chosen opened and exposed a naked female body. Her clean-shaven pubic region suggested a younger woman, but she could have been older. I had no idea of knowing, because only the lower part of her body was exposed.

She came closer, touched my chest and my biceps. Her hands traveled down my body, cupped my testicles. I felt myself reacting to her soft touch. Her breath quickened when my penis grew in her hand. Pressing herself against me, she lifted up on tiptoes, rubbed her clitoris on my erect member. Her breath came in little gasps now, and stepping back she sank to the floor, lay on her back, with her legs pulled up and wide open.

I saw other couples beside us already locked together, naked buttocks moved up and down between spread thighs. I didn't need any more encouragement. Sinking to my knees, I moved between the woman's open legs. She gasped when the tip of my penis touched her labia. I pushed forward, felt myself sliding into her hot and creamy sheath. Lifting her buttocks off the floor, she took me deep into her and began squirming underneath me. She had been more than ready, and it didn't take long for her to reach her first climax. I held back as long as I could, and when I finally came inside her, she had experienced at least half a dozen orgasms.

Someone touched my shoulder. When I looked, I saw two yellow-robed females standing beside me. One grabbed my hand and pulled me up. She pointed to a rectangular cube, which had risen out of the floor. It was clearly an altar. On top of it lay a naked woman. On either side of the altar stood a black-robed priest. The two women led me toward the altar. The woman on top was young, on some worlds she'd be considered underage, just a girl. Between her slightly spread thighs, her hairless vagina beckoned. I knew what they wanted, so when one of the women gave me a gentle push, I stepped up to the altar, positioned myself between the girl's spread legs.

Her sex-organ was just at the right height, and guiding my stiff penis toward it, I slowly entered her already moist sheath. She was tight and gave a little moan when I pushed into her. The priests held her arms, but her lower body was free to move, and soon she began rotating her hips. She cried out when she experienced her first orgasm.

"Let us know when you're ready," a voice whispered into my ear.

I nodded, watching the young woman squirm in my hands, which I had clamped around her moving, narrow hips. Feasting my eyes on her lovely body, I enjoyed the view of her small, but nicely shaped breasts, and her rippling, flat belly. The expression on her pretty, delicate face was one of pure rapture.

"Now!" I called out, and released my built-up pressure.

As I came inside the young woman's clutching organ, the priest on her left lifted her arm, and with a quick motion he drew a knife across her wrist. One of the women knelt beside him and caught the flowing blood in a golden cup. I pulled out, my penis still throbbing, but before I could act, the other priest began wrapping a bandage around the girl's bleeding wrist, stemming the flow of blood. The woman with the filled cup handed it to one of the priests. He pushed back his hood. I recognized Brother Trovar. He lifted the cup to his lips, drank from it, and then he gave it to the other priest, who emptied it. The girl still lay there, her legs open. Someone pulled me away. Another man took my place; I watched him enter the girl's exposed sex-organ, watched him climax inside her. His buttocks quivered as he filled her with his seed. He was a big man, muscular, well-built, and almost as big as I was.

Two more came after him. When they were done, the priests led the young woman away. Out of the group of yellow-robed women one approached the altar. Shrugging out of her robe, she exposed the rest of her body, except her face. She lay down on the altar, pulled up her legs. Her eyes, visible through slits in her veil, were on me.

The woman, who was holding onto my arm, whispered, "Go."

I was still stiff. Moving between her two open thighs, I pushed deep into the warm belly of yet another woman. I didn't rush, made her come several times. She whimpered and cried out each time, her body shaking violently. I became aware of yellow and red robes surrounding us, and I heard the chanting of female and male voices.

When I stopped moving to empty myself into the woman's clenching sheath the chanting rose to a thundering crescendo, drowning out my roar of pleasure.

The woman let out a deep sigh and relaxed her legs. "Thank you for your gift." Her words rang loud in the sudden silence. I pulled out of her, looked around for my robe.

I found it lying on the floor. Flinging it across my shoulders, I followed the group of Red Robes back into the changing room.

After I was dressed, a few men came up to me, clapped me on the shoulder and smiled.

"A great offering," one of them said. "*He* will be pleased."

Sky was waiting for me in the library. She smiled, when I approached, but didn't say anything. Only then I realized that she wasn't wearing her veil. When I lifted an eyebrow, she laughed. "You've seen my face," she said, "we are not that formal around here."

"So why is *your* face covered?" I looked at Skyla.

She chuckled. "You haven't seen my face—yet."

"You mean there is a chance I may see it some day?"

"Maybe," she said coyly and laughed.

Chapter Twenty-eight

When I boarded my Sprayer the next morning, I was surprised to find a new copilot.

A woman--it was obvious: the loose-fitting spraying outfit hid the slim form of her body, but couldn't hide the swell of her breasts. A black breathing mask, instead of a veil, covered her face.

She laughed softly when she saw my surprised look. "I asked my grandfather if I could fly with you today," she said.

Skyla! I should have known.

"I hope you know what you're doing," I said. "This is dangerous work."

"Don't worry, I do. My grandfather taught me well."

We took off. Half an hour later we began spraying and I had to admit, she was a professional. At lunchtime we landed beside a wide river. Skyla had brought a blanket for us to sit on.

Turning away from me, she took off her mask, put on a thin veil.

"Are you afraid I'll recognize you in a crowd?" I asked her.

"I don't understand."

"You always wear a veil. What harm would there be if I saw your face?"

"My religion forbids me." She turned to take a sip from her water bottle.

"Why did you come with me today?" I asked her.

Her gold-flecked eyes studied me. "I needed to talk to you," she said after a long pause.

"About what?"

"About you. About the places you've seen. About other people. I had a talk with those two alien women, Sharina and Kabrina, your companions. They told me things I never knew existed."

I chuckled. "They are not human, Skyla. Their world is even more different from yours than mine."

"I know. That is why I want to talk with you. Tell me about Earth, the birthplace of humanity."

"Earth." I said. "A crowded place. Depleted of all its natural resources. Ravaged by disasters and wars. The air and oceans polluted by industrial waste. Most of the animals extinct. A planet dependent on its colonies. That is Earth."

"It doesn't sound like the world the old, forbidden books describe."

"Your books talk about a world that existed over a thousand years ago. Much has changed since then. Mankind hasn't learned."

"What about religion? I know we've talked about this before, briefly. What do people believe in?"

I shrugged. "There are many religions. Most of them are just variations of the same. All believe in a god, or some kind of deity, but they give him different names. Some believe he is just a force, a vast intelligence without a physical body. Some believe God is a woman. There are others who say God is nothing but a myth, a nice fairy tale, created by men or groups of men to give them power. They believe the Universe runs itself, without any conscious direction."

"You told me that many believe in the Golden God, our god."

"It's true. Seems to me I found where that belief originated. I just can't figure out how it spread to the rest of the Galaxy, when your planet supposedly has no contact with anyone. It strikes me as peculiar."

"Maybe it is because ours is the one and only religion."

I laughed. "Every religion claims that. It has been like that ever since the first man declared himself a shaman or holy man and tried to brainwash his followers into believing that only through him they could get into Paradise. That he was the only one, everyone else was an imposter. Power, Skyla, power."

"You are cynical, Thomas." She looked across the river. We were sitting in the shade of a tall tree. "This is a beautiful spot," she said. "Makes me forget things." She lay back, stared into the sky. "Let's take the afternoon off."

"And do what?"

"Just stay here. Do nothing. The water is warm at this time of year. We could go bathing."

I studied her, lying there on the blanket. "What would Sir Collingdale say? He wouldn't be very happy."

She laughed. "No, he wouldn't be. But who is going to tell him?"

She lifted her head and looked at me. "I'm his granddaughter, remember. That makes me your boss. I've decided it is time for a long rest. Tomorrow we'll work twice as hard."

I shrugged, grinned at her. "Like you said--you're the boss. Maybe I will go swimming. It is hot today."

She watched me as I got undressed, exhaled audibly when she saw me naked. When I looked at her, she turned her head. "I've never seen a man without clothes," she said, "except for the priest who represents the Golden God."

"I'm sorry if I offended you," I apologized.

"You didn't offend me." Her eyes met mine. The visible portion of her face seemed flushed. "You look so…so perfect." The gaze of her eyes dipped to my lower body, lingered for a moment.

I smiled, but didn't move. I've never been shy.

"You are so big," she said. "Everywhere." She blushed even more.

"Are you coming into the water?" I asked.

She shook her head. "Maybe later."

The water was warm, but still refreshing. I swam out into the middle of the river, working against the strong current. Looking back to shore, I saw Skyla watching me. She waived and called something, but I couldn't make out the words. Diving under I swam back. I can hold my breath for a long time and when I surfaced, I was quite close to land. Wiping my eyes, I searched for Skyla and was surprised to see her standing knee-deep in the water, not far from me.

Water dripped from her nude body. Her long, black hair hung loose around her shoulders, partially covering her breasts. But I saw enough of her to make me inhale sharply. Her gold-flecked eyes seemed to laugh at me and for the first time I saw her smile. "Hello, Thomas," she said with a low voice.

I rose up in front of her, recognition flooding through me. "You are the dancer from the temple," I said. "The High Priestess."

"The dancer--yes, but not the High Priestess. Not yet." Her smile vanished. "I don't want to be the High Priestess."

"Why not?"

"In two quarter-cycles I will join with the Golden God. He will impregnate me and I will bear his son. Only it is not the Golden God who will put his seed into my womb, but a lowly priest." She stepped up to me, her breasts almost touching me. Her golden eyes flickered as she searched my face. There was a rosy color on her cheeks as she spoke. "If I loose my virginity before then I would be considered spoiled. I want you to take my virginity, Thomas."

"Do you know what you are asking?"

She nodded fiercely. "I've given it a lot of thought, even before you came here. I never wanted to be a High Priestess. It was my father's idea. I've asked the Golden God for help, and when I saw you for the first time, I knew you were the one."

"Another legend?" I asked.

"Legend? Explain."

I chuckled. "Never mind. I don't know if this is such a good idea. You are so young."

She put her arms around my neck, kissed me. Her lips were warm and yielding. I felt her soft breasts against my chest, and then the rest of her nubile body.

"I am a fully grown woman, Thomas. I have friends my age who are mothers already. Had I not been chosen to be a High Priestess my virginity may not me intact anymore. Do you find me unattractive?"

My hand had moved down to her round buttocks. They felt soft, and yet solid. They quivered gently in my hands. "You are one of the most beautiful women I have ever seen," I told her. "And I find you incredibly attractive."

She twisted out of my arms, took my hand and pulled me onto land, where she lay down in the grass. "Come," she said, smiling up at me. "I know it will hurt a little, but I am not afraid."

"I'll be gentle," I said, dropping down beside her. I parted her hair, which had fallen over her face and studied her lovely features. I had been smitten with her beauty when I saw her dance in the temple. She was even more beautiful close-up. I kissed her and ran my hands over her gorgeous body. She was slim, but not skinny. Muscular, without showing it. Her breasts were large and firm, with thick nipples; her pubis covered with a black triangle of hair.

Stroking her vulva, I put my finger into her slit, rubbed her clitoris, until she moaned. When she was ready, I lay on top of her, opened her legs with my hands. She cried out when I entered her, breaking her hymen with a forceful thrust. "Shh…" I whispered, stroking her cheek. "Relax."

She experienced her first orgasm long before I had mine. I wanted to pull out, but her hands clasped my buttocks, held me in a strong grip. Shuddering, I emptied myself, filling her young womb with my seed.

"If it is the Golden God's wish I will bear your son," she whispered, and added, "Rather yours than the priest's."

Afterwards she lay in my arms, snuggled against me. "I've never met anyone like you, Thomas. You don't seem to be afraid of anything, but you don't swagger around either, showing off your strength and braveness. My mother told me again how you killed those three Guardian Enforcers, with just your knife." She looked into my eyes. Her finger traced my lips. "Are you a god, Thomas?"

I laughed and stroked her hair. "Would a god waste his time spraying Seedjumpers?"

She shrugged. "I don't know what gods do in their spare time." Planting a quick kiss on my lips, she squirmed out of my embrace and rose to her feet. "I'm going to cool off."

I watched her plump buttocks dance as she ran toward the river. She had beautifully formed long legs. The water splashed as she dove into it. I closed my eyes for a moment and must have dozed off.

* * * *

He stood there, more lifelike than ever. His golden wings trailed on the marble floor. I saw two suns behind him, one bright, the other one like a red giant eye.

Beside him stood a young man, dressed in a black uniform. In his hands he held what looked like a flamethrower.

The young man looked at me. He was handsome, arrogant in his manner. "Hello, Father," he said.

"I don't know you," I said.

He smiled. "And you never will. But I know you."

"Look at him closely," said the golden man. "He will be hailed as a god, the Savior, but he will bring chaos to Ramarra. The rule of the Church will be broken and there will be anarchy--until your son assumes control. He will be a ruthless leader.

There will be a war with Arenia, and many will die. After that he will use the gates to invade other worlds. His ambition: to create an empire."

I shrugged. "Empires come and go. They never last."

"The Guardians will have to interfere--again."

"The Guardians!" I sneered. "What gives them the right?"

"It is not a question of right or wrong. They have no choice. Everything must balance, otherwise there would be nothing but chaos."

"Would that be so bad?" I asked.

He smiled. "I did not expect you to say anything different. After all--you are the Lord of Chaos."

I laughed and spread my wings. Soaring into the sky, I rose higher and higher, until the world was nothing but a giant globe hanging in the blackness of space.

"Let there be Chaos!" My laughter filled the void, echoed between the worlds.

"Let there be Chaos!"

* * * *

I awoke, drenched in sweat. Skyla stood above me, her naked body glistening wetly in the bright sun. "Were you sleeping?" she asked.

I shook my head to clear away the remnants of my nightmare. "You tired me out." I smiled up at her. She looked so beautiful.

She straddled me and lowered herself. Sitting on my thighs, she played with my penis, fondled it until it was a hard rod. Then she slid forward. I felt myself entering her moist and tight hot sheath. Rotating her pelvis, she smiled happily.

"What happened to my innocent virgin?" I asked.

She laughed, milking me fiercely. "Gone for good," she breathed, and cried out when a powerful climax gripped her body.

I should have felt guilty for despoiling a virgin, but I didn't. It would have happened eventually. This girl had been a volcano ready to explode at any time. Maybe it was a good thing I was the one who lit the torch. The priest might have damaged her wild and free spirit forever.

I grabbed her slim hips, lunged upwards as my own climax approached. She laughed when she felt my discharge, quivered suddenly and began to sob as the pleasure of her orgasm overwhelmed her. After that she rode me with wild recklessness for a long time.

When her desire was satisfied, we went into the water to cool off and clean our sweaty bodies.

I never heard them come.

As silent as a flock of birds they landed beside our Flyer. Three sleek black aircraft. The symbol of the Golden God emblazoned on their hulls.

The Guardian Enforcers had found me.

Chapter Twenty-nine

I counted eighteen men, all dressed in black uniforms, carrying heavy weapons. The pilots had positioned the three aircraft with their noses pointing in my direction; long, narrow tubes moved silently on top of the black roofs, tracking my every movement.

I should have been flattered by this show of power. These guys must really be afraid of me.

"Thomas Reginald Stone?" said their leader as he approached me. His men lined up behind him in a semicircle, their weapons aimed at me.

I tried to smile. "You know who I am. I don't think I need to identify myself."

His expression never changed. "You are under arrest. Do not resist. We have orders to shoot to kill."

"What are the charges?"

"You will be told in good time. Please, turn around!"

"So you can shoot me in the back?"

"If we wanted to shoot you we would have done that already. Don't make this difficult. Now--turn around!"

I looked down at myself. "Can I at least get dressed?"

They gave me time to put on my clothes, then they pulled my arms behind my back and put magnetic holds on my wrists. I didn't even have time to say goodbye to Skyla.

I was marched into one of the aircraft and hauled into the hold, where two Enforcers pushed me into a small cubicle. My body was held prisoner by the force of a magnetic field. It paralyzed me. I couldn't move a muscle.

The Darkness inside me started to rise, but I managed to suppress the impulse, something that surprised me. I'd never been able to do that. I guess my situation was not quite as precarious is it looked, which didn't make me feel any better. Had I managed somehow to escape my prison, where would I have gone?

My mind was still clear, but the influence of the magnetic field slowly began to dull it and I drifted off into what seemed a slow moving world, like a dark lucid dream.

* * * *

"State your name and rank!"

"Kelvin Byrne. Lieutenant."

"What is your position on the Patrol Ship *Barracuda?*"

"Communications officer, sir."

"So you were present when the colony-ship *Hope* was destroyed?" Admiral Sasmussen's deep voice sounded almost pleasant as he questioned my officer.

"Yes, sir, I was."

"You were also present when Commodore Stone decided to ignore his orders?"

"Yes, sir. His orders were…"

"Answer only the question, Lieutenant," the admiral interrupted him. He walked away with a theatrical gesture. Turning around, he asked, "How long have you been under the command of Commodore Stone?"

"Seven years, sir. He was my superior officer when he was still Captain."

"So you're quite loyal to him, wouldn't you say?" Sasmussen stared at him out of dark eyes.

"Yes, sir."

"You would do anything to protect him?"

"Yes, sir."

"Even lie?"

Byrne was silent for a moment, his eyes found mine. "I prefer not to answer that question, sir."

Admiral Sasmussen pointed an accusing finger. "You just did." He turned away. "No further questions."

"Sir, I haven't lied--yet."

"No further questions. Dismissed!"

Byrne looked at me, shrugged and left the witness stand. Then they brought out Slieman, then Roberts, and Slovaki.

Lt. Newcombe, my *Second-in-command*, was the last one. There was something wrong with him. He looked drawn; his eyes seemed to stare into emptiness.

After stating his name and rank, he sat down, his eyes downcast.

"Lieutenant Newcombe, please tell the court in your own words what transpired on the Patrol Ship *Barracuda* on the day in question!"

"After opening the sealed orders Commodore Stone exclaimed *Someone fucked up. That is not a colony ship. That ship carries soldiers. We must destroy it. I will take full responsibility.* Then he gave the order to fire upon the starship *Hope.*"

"Did you see any black delta shaped ships, Lieutenant

Newcombe?"

"No, sir, I didn't." His voice sounded like the voice of an automaton.

Those sons-of-bitches! They had tampered with his mind. This was not the Lieutenant Newcombe I knew. He would never have lied about the incident. Our sealed orders had been *Search and Destroy*, but I had disobeyed that order.

"That is not what happened!" I shouted and rose in my seat.

"One more outburst from you and I will end the trial right here!" Admiral Sasmussen's voice was cold as his eyes.

"Trial!" I sneered. "This is a circus, not a trial."

"Enough!" he roared. "Take the prisoner away!"

* * * *

It took me a moment to realize that the stasis field had been disconnected and I was free to step out of the cubicle. A couple of guards led me away. Their black uniforms displayed the picture of the Golden God, not the red symbol of the atom inside a circle on the blue and white uniform of the Terran Space Navy.

My mind jumped back to the present. I was a prisoner, not on Terra, but on an alien planet. About to face another trial.

I was taken into a black foreboding looking building, then down below ground where they put me into a dark, damp cell. Then they stripped me naked, and to further humiliate me they put chains on my ankles and wrists. Actual chains.

I didn't think anyone did that anymore.

Chapter Thirty

Incarcerated—again.

I was developing a pattern. But this time was much more serious. I wouldn't be able to talk or bluff myself out of this one.

Three days in a dark cell, without food or water, until I was hauled outside. Naked and filthy, without a stitch of clothing, not even my boots, I appeared in front of a group of dark-robed judges.

Their speaker, a thin, haggard looking man, gave me a long stare. He reminded me of Admiral Sasmussen. "We have opened our arms to you in friendship by offering to repair your damaged ship. You were given an opportunity to work off your debt in a fair trade. And how did you repay our kindness?"

I could almost see flames shooting from his eyes when he pointed an accusing finger at me.

"You committed the most heinous crime. You murdered three of our valued citizens--three Guardian Enforcers. Three men who were only doing their job serving their country, their church, and their god. And you murdered them in cold blood. But that is not the only crime you are guilty of. You committed a sacrilege almost worse than the murder of those three good men."

He paused, took a deep breath.

"There is no honor greater than the one that would have been bestowed on one of our privileged young virgins: the honor of being chosen to bear the son of the Golden God. To become his *High Priestess*.

"You took that away from her when you forced yourself on her innocent young body, when you invaded her flesh and her mind."

He walked across the room. His black cloak opened behind him like the wings of a giant bat. Making a dramatic turn he came striding back toward me, one arm raised. "But that is not all. We know now that your coming here was part of a sinister plot to invade our planet."

At that I had to laugh. "I am hardly in a position to invade your planet," I said.

He glared at me. "How else would an armada of warships have found us?"

"I have no idea what you're talking about."

He managed to bark a short laugh. "You don't? Why then would they inquire about you?"

"Like I said, I don't know."

"Don't pretend to be ignorant. You are Thomas Stone, aren't you? Commodore Thomas Reginald Stone?"

"I won't deny that. But I know nothing about an invading force."

"Then you are lying!" he spat and turned to the four guards who had brought me. "Take him back to his cell."

Sitting naked on the hard bench in my cold, dark prison, I had time to contemplate my situation.

What the hell was going on? How had they found out about me? Who had sent warships after me--and why?

Damn! I was hungry, thirsty, and chilled to the bone.

Pacing back and forth, I went to the gate and rapped my hand across the iron bars. "Food and water!" I yelled. "I want some food and water!"

I might as well have saved my efforts for the results my ranting achieved. Taking a deep breath, I inhaled the musky air. There was nobody else around. I was the only prisoner. Judging by the dampness and the fetid odor, I was in an underground tunnel that had been converted into a prison. There was no light in my cell. The only illumination came from a wall fixture about a hundred meters further down.

I lay down on the narrow cold bench and made myself as comfortable as was possible.

They knew about the three Enforcers I had killed. How? Supposedly, that part of the park was not under surveillance. Obviously, that assumption had been wrong. Somehow I had the feeling Raktar had a hand in this. There was no doubt he knew about Sky and me. Now I had screwed his daughter, who would have become a High Priestess. Not only had I despoiled his daughter, I had also foiled his rise in the hierarchy of the Church.

I had managed to do exactly what I wanted to avoid--make an enemy of a person with influence.

Things did not look good.

A noise from the far side of the tunnel made me sit up. Light streamed in, kept coming closer. I heard the footsteps of two people. The door to me cell swung open and a woman walked in.

"Leave us alone," she told the guard. I recognized Sky's voice.

"Is that wise, my Lady?" The guard hesitated. "He is a dangerous criminal."

"I'll be fine," Sky said. "He won't harm me."

She waited until the guard was gone, then she removed her veil and came into my arms.

"How did they find out?" I asked.

She stepped back, looked at me with her brown eyes. "I'm afraid it is my fault. My husband gave me his word that you would get a fair trial if I told what exactly happened. He made only one condition: not to mention his name. He said there were witnesses, and if I didn't tell my side of the story, freely, then we both would be found guilty. I was tricked, I'm sorry."

"You're still free," I said.

"Free--yes. But I may not be alive tomorrow."

"You've been threatened?"

"Not directly. But I have lost my usefulness to my husband. He will have me killed."

"What's all this about an armada of warships?" I asked.

"Two days ago a huge ship dropped out of warped space inside our defense-net. It was followed by four smaller, heavily armed vessels. A swarm of small, but deadly fighters appeared out of the huge ship's belly; they destroyed much of our fleet. We were taken by surprise. They gave us an ultimatum. I don't know the details. The Guardian Council does not share information with the citizens of Ramarra, unless it is absolutely necessary."

"How do *you* know all of this?"

She smiled. "I have friends in the space force."

"Apparently someone asked for me," I said.

She shook her head. "I don't know about that." Staring into my face she asked, "Do you have anything to do with this?"

"No. Unless I have more information I wouldn't even make any assumptions." It was my turn to search her face. "Can you get me out of here?"

"I'm afraid not. I was lucky they let me in to see you."

"I don't think it was luck," I said. As if to confirm my suspicion, the door at the far end opened and a group of armed guards came rushing down the corridor.

"Get away from the prisoner!" someone barked.

Sky moved away from me, frightened.

There were at least a dozen of them. They covered me with their weapons, told me to come out of the cell, slowly.

I obliged them. I *did* count twelve guards. They really must fear me. Six walked ahead, six behind me, their weapons aimed at my back.

I was herded down another corridor, into a room. In one wall I recognized the outlines of a Gate. They pushed me through it. On the other side I was received by six more guards. They stood in line, weapons trained at me.

They sure weren't taking any chances.

We were underground. In a cavern similar to the one under the temple. There were statues and carvings on the walls. Faded paintings on the ceiling. In the center, on a raised dais, stood the Golden God, sword in hand. Behind him the shimmering field of a giant Portal.

Something was different in this room. I could feel the energy that emanated from the Gate. It entered my body, my mind. The Darkness inside me began to gather. I felt uneasy, anxious.

There was another statue, not far from the Golden God. A strong pulling in my head made me walk toward it. They didn't stop me.

He looked as if he would step down from his pedestal at any moment. His golden body was magnificent. His face handsome, arrogant. Familiar. His wings were half-spread, like a black, velvety cloak.

"We finally meet," I whispered.

I turned around when I heard the commotion behind me. Out of the Gate at the far end streamed a number of armed soldiers. They didn't wear black, but white uniforms. I recognized them, recognized the red and blue symbol of the Colonial Worlds on the chest of the soldiers; something I had not expected to see here.

There were other uniforms among them. Uniforms I couldn't identify. But I knew two of the people wearing these uniforms. I should have known they were involved. One of them came running, smiled when she was close.

"Hello, Thomas."

"Sharina," I said. "I see you brought friends."

"A few. We thought you needed help."

I watched the man who came slowly walking toward us. "Colonel Voltaire," I said, when he stopped beside Sharina.

He saluted. "Commodore Stone. I'm glad you are alive and fairly well."

"How did you find me?" I asked.

He smiled thinly. "That tiny thing in your head--it's not really a bomb. It is a tracking device. A little marvel our new friends supplied." He indicated Sharina.

She shrugged. "I admit our technology is a bit more advanced than yours." She looked at me. "We had that tracker put into your head strictly as insurance. In case you managed to loose us. But it wasn't really necessary; we had our own means of contacting our people."

"Why?" I asked.

"Thomas, Thomas. You can't be that ignorant. We may be far advanced, but there are things even we don't possess. I'm talking about the Portals. We knew they existed, but we didn't know where."

"Now you've found them."

Before she could comment, we were interrupted by the arrival of more people. This time they appeared out of another Gate.

Guardian Enforcers, four of them. Between them they held two prisoners. Two women, their faces without a covering.

Sky and her daughter Skyla.

When Skyla saw me, she struggled and managed to free herself from her captors. Running toward me, she called, "Tell them who you really are."

"By now everybody knows who I am. I am Thomas Stone, Commodore Thomas Reginald Stone." I smiled at her. "Who else would I be?"

She fell to her knees in front of me, kissed my feet. Then she looked up and smiled.

"Welcome home."

"What is she babbling about?" Sharina demanded to know.

"Don't you recognize him?" Skyla asked. "Look at the statue. Look at him."

Sharina laughed. "So there is a resemblance. It means nothing. He is who he says he is--nothing more. We've spent much time with him, we know him better than anyone else." She looked at me. "Be a good boy, Thomas, and step aside, so we can examine the Portal."

Out of the second Gate jumped more armed Guardian Enforcers. Among them a familiar figure. His gaunt features were not easily forgotten. He lifted his hand. "Don't shoot," he called to the Colonial Marines.

"And who might you be?" Colonel Voltaire asked.

"I am Admiral Asmussen."

"You are wearing the uniform of the Terran Space Navy."

The admiral smiled. "That is correct, but my home world is Ramarra, the planet you are invading."

"I see. A traitor to the human race," Voltaire sneered.

"Not a traitor. I am human myself, at least half, anyway." The admiral looked at me. "I tried to keep you away from here, but I see I was not successful. Now you are here, and you brought the invaders with you. It is your fault that the Ra-el-marras have failed. The secret of the Portals was never to be revealed."

"Well, Admiral, it is too late for that." Sharina said. "We've searched for these Portals for a long time. Now that we've found them, we won't leave." Again she looked at me. "Poor Thomas. You've been a pawn, and you didn't know it. If it's any consolation--Kabrina and I were quite fond of you. But now you've lost your usefulness. So let us pass!"

"You are committing a great sacrilege," Skyla said. "You claim to know him, but you don't."

Sharina glared at her with contempt. "Who do you think he is, little girl?"

"He is the son of the Golden God. He came here to claim his birthright."

Sharina laughed and looked at me. "Are you his son, Thomas?"

Behind me the Portal began to emit a bright light. I didn't have to turn around to see it. Inside me the *Light* and the *Darkness* merged.

I smiled.

"No, I am not his son," I said and let the transformation ripple through my body.

Chapter Thirty-one

Looking down at my golden skin, I spread my wings, exulted in the feeling of being whole again. I remembered.Millennia of existence. Endless identities on countless planets throughout the Galaxy. Centuries of living on Earth, the cradle of humankind.

A chief in a tribe of primates. A medicine man.

A philosopher in ancient Greece. A warrior in Sparta.

A priest in Egypt. A Pharaoh.

Forty years in the desert with a tribe of nomads.

A senator in Rome.

A warlord conquering the steppes of Asia and Europe with the hordes of Genghis Khan.

An advisor to Napoleon.

A high-ranking officer in the Third Reich.

An assassin hunting terrorists in the 21st century.

Ambassador to Nova Terra, the first independent Earth colony.

A colonel with the Terran Space Force, fighting the Insectoids on Sirius *V*.

Moving from identity to identity. Never aging. Never knowing who I really was.

Always forgetting. I remembered--if only for a short time.

* * * *

They stepped through the Portal, as I knew they would.

Gabriel and Raphael.

Folding my black wings behind me, I turned to look at them. "Greetings, my brothers," I said, not with my mouth, but with my mind.

"You cannot enter," Gabriel said.

They carried long, flaming swords in their golden hands; but those were only symbols of their status. Golden wings half-spread, they looked at me with sadness in their burning eyes.

Sadness and love.

"It's been so long," I said.

"Not long enough," Raphael said softly.

"How long still?" I asked.

Gabriel shook his golden head. "Only the Guardians know."

"Will there be an end?"

"An end to Chaos? Yes. Until the cycle begins anew." Gabriel's thoughts seemed harsh. "You wanted to reign."

"Not like this. Not hiding in the dark recesses of my own mind. Never able to experience my full glory. Never to be who I really am."

"That was of your own choosing. Had you remained inside your intended prison time would have been only a moment. But you were clever, you escaped."

"Why did the Guardians not search for me?"

Raphael laughed. "They have their own reasons. Maybe you were an experiment. Maybe they wanted to find out what results when Chaos rules."

"Perhaps this was all meant to be," I said.

"Perhaps."

"What is going to happen next?" I asked, my eyes sweeping the assembled crowd. Humans. Ra-el-marras. Karpaas.

They stood like statues, frozen in time.

"They will take the secret of the Gates with them, but nothing will really change. They will pray to the Golden God, like before, waiting for his return. Maybe they will create a new religion. What does it matter?"

The Portal exploded into myriads of lights. The awesome power of the Guardian flooded the cavern. He had no physical substance, no body. He couldn't be seen, but he was there. He just--was.

He didn't speak, but I was filled with his words. I understood and I accepted. His Word was Law.

"I must go," I said to Gabriel and Raphael.

"Where will you go?"

"Back to rule Chaos, until the cycle ends," I said.

They both nodded.

"Until then, Lucifer."

The End